Wolf at the Door

A W.D. CALDWELL MYSTERY

JOANNA DYMOND

THE BIRCHTREE PUBLISHING GROUP, LTD.
P.O. BOX 1644
BEMIDJI, MINNESOTA 56619

WOLF AT THE DOOR
COPYRIGHT © 2021 by Joanna Dymond. All rights reserved.

This is a work of fiction. Names, characters, places, incidents or events; either are the products of the author's imagination or are used fictitiously, and any resemblance to actual persons, living or dead, former or current business establishments, events, or locales, is entirely coincidental.

"The Catastrophe of Success" quote copyright © 1947 by Tennessee Williams.

Cover design: Connie Knutson and Joanna Dymond.
Cover design copyright © 2021 Birchtree Publishing Group Ltd.

No part of this book may be reproduced, scanned, or distributed in any printed, electronic, mechanical, or spoken form without written permission from the author. Please do not participate in or encourage piracy of copyrighted materials in violation of the author's rights. Purchase only authorized editions.

All subsidiary rights to *Wolf at the Door* including eBook, Film ,TV, and Audio Book are owned by Birchtree Publishing Group Ltd and can be contacted at PO Box 1644, Bemidji, MN 56619.

For information or to place orders, write to:
Birchtree Publishing Group Ltd
P.O. Box 1644, Bemidji, Minnesota 56619 USA
218-751-7722
www.joannadymond.com

Library of Congress Control Number: 2015908128

ISBN: 978-0-578-84736-8

Birchtree Books are published by Birchtree Publishing Group LTD, a division of Birchtree Acres Inc. Its trademarks consists of three birchtree on the property owned by the author with a logo "Time is more precious than money, more precious than the most valuable thing in the world," and is registered in the U.S. Patent and Trademark Office, 2021.
Only books with this trademark are legally sold in the United States.

Printed in the United States of America 2021

1 2 3 4 5 6 7 8 9 10

This book is dedicated to my Three Best Friends Forever.

Sharon Day
Susan Sternfels
Twilah Klemmetsen
I miss you all very much

"Time is more precious than money, more precious than the most valuable thing in the world."

BIRCHTREE PUBLISHING GROUP, LTD.
WALTER MEDEIROS, PRESIDENT
P.O. BOX 1644, BEMIDJI, MINNESOTA 56619
218.751.7722
CORPORATE ID#41 167491

Dear Readers,

My book title is somewhat inspired by Tennessee Williams' essay entitled "The Catastrophe of Success" published in the *New York Times* in 1947 and the title is related to a quote from this essay "…that not privation but luxury is the **wolf at the door** and that the fangs of this wolf are the little vanities and conceits and laxities that Success is heir to…."

Copyright © 1947 Tennessee Williams

Joanna Dymond

PROLOGUE

Excerpt from a 9:00 a.m. introductory speech presented by Dr. Aldean Matheson, guest lecturer and bestselling author, at an annual workshop for MFA candidates at the Stony Brook Southampton 1988 Writers Conference.

"Good morning, my fellow writers, I'll get right to it. On your chair you will find a copy of my latest book, *The Scandalous Odyssey of an Oil Tycoon*. Please open to page five where you will find a detailed map of Los Angeles.

When I first started researching this book, I was stunned by how little I knew about one of our greatest cities. I had, like many people, bought the image of Los Angeles as the mecca of entertainment. I also thought of it as the center of health and physical fitness. Didn't some of the most beautiful specimens of humankind choose to live there? Also I bought the legend of a perfect climate, palm trees, and cool ocean breezes.

But I'm not going to break this to you gently. This wonderful Southern California locale is the third largest oil producing site in the USA. Well, so what, you ask?

Well, this oil is coming from derricks and pump jacks in the Los Angeles Basin, San Joaquin Valley, and Kern County. Now, let me be more precise. The City of Los Angeles is a gigantic oil field and has been since the late 19th century! In 1856, a company began working the tar pits at Rancho La

Brea, later drilling some oil out of there. In 1890, Edward L. Doheny discovered the Los Angeles City Oil Field and in 1892, he discovered oil in downtown L.A., becoming one of the richest men in California. Oh, it's a long story and you can read my book.

My ultimate conclusion is quite harsh: Los Angeles has lived a lie since 1892. It has been a big secret that it's oil rich. The derricks and pump jacks are skillfully and artfully disguised behind fake walls, and phony mini malls. They pump night and day and are very near or next to schools, hospitals, apartment buildings, churches, synagogues, mosques, and residential neighborhoods. They spew a stinky poisonous gas, due to a fracking system, making people ill, many terminally so. The air, the drinking water, and the food grown in that soil have caused unexplained health issues and the public is unaware of the oil production field in their daily lives. In the big picture, huge oil money profits could and do impact crime. In 1988, the violent crime statistics for L.A. County are surprising and they are not always drug-related.

So in conclusion, my friends…ah…read my b-b-book and s-s-s-share my agony." His stutter had returned.

Dr. Matheson abruptly walked off the stage. He did not look back as the room erupted in clapping, cheering, and huzzahs. He took off running from the back exit toward an idling silver Porsche 928. He got into the passenger side, his assistant at the wheel. "G-G-Good to see you Stella," he said, "the medication is wearing off." She shifted down, stepped on the gas and headed to Montauk.

Their day had just begun.

1

"Good morning, Mr. Swinburne," said the guard. "Welcome to Environ-Oil…ah, your cousin's not in yet, sir."

"Oh, I'm a little early," smiled R. Proctor Swinburne.

He pulled his Lotus Esprit into the VIP parking area of Environ-Oil and Refinery, glad to be at the company before the staff arrived. He held out his ID for security, parked and stepped out of the car and into the entrance of the reception area. He noiselessly made his way to the coffee room and then on to the low light, plush conference room. He was the CEO and major shareholder of Environ-Oil, inheriting the company from his father and his grandfather before him. He ran the business with his cousin Ben, who acted as president.

The company was situated outside Oxnard, California, in a gated community. He set his briefcase down and rolled out a chair. He looked around the room as he sipped his coffee. He examined the wall and the exquisitely expensive prints that comprised his late father Russell Swinburne's art collection hanging among the many industry awards.

He thought fondly of the family business: Oil, a black sludge, smelly, infiltrating one's skin. It was hard to escape its presence. One could not admire it. Yet, it was more valuable than just about any commodity on earth.

Swinburne's eyes swept across a U.S. pipeline map, huge and beautifully designed. He looked a second time more closely, staring at the red, blue, and yellow pipeline patterns. He saw that the pipeline terminal in Clearbrook, Minnesota served five from the west, four from the east, and two from the south.

This greatly piqued his interest. He walked over to the front of the map, using his finger as a pointer to trace the pipeline route. This map was the reason he'd opened a branch office in St. Paul. While many people had never heard of Clearbrook, Swinburne watched what happened there closely. He knew it could someday become a game changer, perhaps becoming a market hub for crude oil.

The Clearbrook distribution terminal was built in 1950 and had been expanded many times over the decades, serving as a major gateway for oil flowing from Canada across the USA to the Gulf Coast. The oil that flowed underneath the ground was mostly unseen by the farming community. But they had been hard hit by a recession in the 1980's and many of them sold out to the pipeline companies. Farming as an occupation became a thing of the past in Northwest Minnesota.

Proctor was proud of the family business. They were independent oilmen operating since the 1920's on hills overlooking various neighborhoods in downtown Los Angeles. In recent years, Environ-Oil had cut back to 54 oil derricks and 14 storage tanks in Signal Hill and ten derricks and four storage tanks in the LaBrea neighborhood. Both locations were under round-the-clock surveillance by video cameras mounted on 45-foot poles.

They managed their employees by having them clock into fenced-in trailer parks near the two locations. The times had changed since the early days and now secrecy and outright deception was necessary. Oil extraction was big business and derricks and pump jacks once situated in plain sight, near homes, schools, golf courses, and even orange groves, now had to be camouflaged with palm trees and waterfalls, placed inside windowless office buildings, fake mini-malls and disguised synagogues.

He reached for the extension telephone and dialed the office manager. "Good morning, Sirina, is Ben in yet? No? Okay. In the meantime I'd like Joyce to join me in the conference room for some dictation – I have several letters to go off this morning by Fax."

A few minutes later the beautiful Joyce Santa Anna appeared in the doorway. "Good morning, sir. I'm ready for dictation. Ah, would you like a refill of your coffee?"

"Oh, yes. Say, Joyce, after I dictate these letters, I want you to do some research for me."

"Of course, I'd be delighted." She shook her head slowly, accentuating her well-groomed and recently brushed long black hair. She was dressed in a crisp white blouse and a black pencil skirt, her thin, delicate frame enhanced by the simple lines.

After signing the letters, he gave her the Fax numbers from his Day-Timer, and then went into detail on the research.

"Now, I need you to find out how much property is for sale in northwest Minnesota, near a small town called Trail." He stroked his knuckles as he spoke. "I need, maybe, 1000-1200 acres in Gully Township – this is near Clearbook. If there's a realtor listed, get his name, and asking price."

"Yes sir." Joyce immediately left the office, ready to do his bidding.

#   #   #

He planned to buy up land in northwest Minnesota to build a terminal for another pipeline he knew was coming. Didn't Minnesota have a policy of closely following existing pipelines when new ones were permitted and built? He was serious about leaving his mark on the global oil industry and making his first billion dollars.

Later that afternoon Joyce knocked on the conference room door where Swinburne had been reviewing some contracts.

"I've got some information, sir."

"Come in," said Swinburne, his excitement barely contained.

"Within the last month, 1,280 acres came up for sale in the Gully and Johnson Townships. It's the estate of a deceased individual named Steve Olsen. The land is comprised of two sections of 640 acres each, abutted by state land on one side and on the other environmentally sensitive acreage." She picked up a piece of paper and read it. "It's being handled by a realtor named W.D. Caldwell who has an office in Erskine, Minnesota. He's showing the property and taking bids."

"What's the asking or starting price?"

"Uh, none listed."

"Hmm, find out the appraised value from the courthouse. After that, I guess I'll just make a bid…that property should be cheap to buy since its part of an estate."

"Well, no, not really. It seems the land has gone through probate and an auction already held. Mr. Caldwell bought everything – the property, house, outbuildings, all the furnishings, outdoor equipment, indoor appliances, a sports ATV, two cars, and an airplane. A big drawback is that there is only a small road, like a trail, going in there. Caldwell's the one who has it up for sale."

"Huh?" Swinburne sat back in his chair and thought for a few moments. "Oh, I'm pretty sure this realtor must be some kind of hick – living there in the sticks. I'll make him an offer so high that it'll blow his pants off."

Swinburne started to laugh. He was going to have some fun. Oh, my, yes!

2

W.D. Caldwell, a local real estate broker drove his new 1989 Taurus into the Caldwell Real Estate parking lot close to the steps of the front door. It was a log cabin office and fit the rural surroundings of Erskine in northwest Minnesota. His wife Renee was already there because she had some typing to do for an upcoming sale.

W.D. wore his cowboy boots today. For being 75 years old, he had surprisingly good posture, and his faded Levis, pressed with a crease, were belted with a big buckle that had the initials H.L. on it. The rodeo trophy buckle had belonged to his father Henning Leroy Caldwell, a professional rodeo calf roper who had won the buckle at the Minnesota State Fair Rodeo in 1949.

"Hi honey," W.D. greeted his wife with a smile and glanced at the coffee pot.

"Hi dear, let me get you a cup of coffee. It's already been a busy morning." She sighed as she pulled his pottery cup off the hook with the slogan "Advice from a Wolf" on it.

"Why's that?" he asked. He sat down at his desk and started to light up one of his *Romeo y Julieta* cigars.

"Well, a man has called twice for you from California.

Says it's very important. It seems he wants to buy that 1,280 acre wilderness property in Gully Township."

"Oh yeah, I've been over there scoping it out. Even hired a pilot to fly me over the land." He looked out the window at the young aspen tree he'd planted that spring. "It's a fantastic piece of property."

W.D. had recently purchased it from an estate sale. He thought of the former owner, the late Steve Olsen, a drug dealer who'd been killed in a home invasion.

"What are the main features and what do you think you can price out the acreage for?"

"Well, I don't know – I guess it's a bit of everything – wetlands, timber, some tillable land, two small lakes for fishing, and the Lost River crosses it."

"Hmm, very impressive – got a price yet?"

"Yeah, well, maybe $500.00 an acre. Maybe more."

The telephone rang and W.D. picked it up.

"W.D. Caldwell, the best real estate agent in Minnesota – I sell more in a month than others do in a year. What can I do for you?"

A deep voice chuckled and then said hello, seemingly enjoying W.D.'s self plug. "Well, I guess I got the right place. My name's Proctor Swinburne and I read about those 1,280 acres you have for sale up in Gully Township. Would you take a bank wire transfer?"

"Hey, hold on, sir, I don't even know who you are. Could you tell me about yourself? Also I already have two bids on that land."

Suddenly the man's voice became steely. "I've got to have that land, Mr. Real Estate Man and I'll pay more than the asking price – whatever that is. Also I want to buy right away, sight unseen."

"First of all, my name is not Mr. Real Estate Man, it's W.D. Caldwell and if we are to do any further conversing, I insist you use it." W.D. was surprised by the offer to pay more than the asking price. Who does that if they don't even know what it is?

"My apologies, Mr. Caldwell, I just got carried away. Yes, let me tell you a bit about myself. I live in California and am in the entertainment business. We own several RV campgrounds in Southern California and employ around 500 people. We are now branching out of state and are looking at buying land in Montana, North Dakota, and Minnesota." He lied extremely well.

"Yes, I see. It would make a good landscape for RV camping and hiking. Ah, there's no roads in there except a trail up to the house. Well, I would advise you to make a trip here to Minnesota and meet with me so I can show you the property. I'll have my pilot fly us over it." W.D. thought of the big expense of building roads in there. "When would you like to visit?"

"I wouldn't. I can't get away. I may have to send my secretary."

"Hmm. I see. Well, sir, that's not good enough. You must appear in person, fill out an application, and be subject to a criminal check as well as providing your proof of funds. If that's not possible there will be no sale. Thank you for your inquiry." He hung up.

W.D. sat back in his leather chair and wondered what kind of business man he'd just talked to. There was something strange about his desperate effort to buy the property sight unseen. Send his secretary? To buy the property? It would never happen. He didn't sell to secretaries. Sometimes he didn't even sell to someone who played by all the rules.

"Hon, are you ready for our upcoming trip to Los Angeles?" W.D smiled at his wife, who still had her head bent over her typewriter. Even though they had a top of the line computer processor, she still liked to type on a manual. "I can't get over that invitation from CBS Television and that director, can you?"

"Oh, no, I can barely believe it. They must think you're a Special Agent? Anyway, I just had my hair cut and colored yesterday at Berta's Salon. I need to buy a pair of white slacks somewhere."

The telephone rang again and W.D. picked it up.

"Good morning, W.D. Caldwell. This is the number one real estate office in Minnesota. What can I do for you?"

"Good morning, Mr. Caldwell, my name is Joyce Santa Anna and I would like to put in a bid for that 1,000 acre wilderness property I read about. Is it still available?"

"Yes, it is, Mrs. Santa Anna, but its 1,280 acres – two sections. Please tell me a bit about yourself. For instance, do you plan to live there?"

"Well, I live in Malibu, California; I'm a teacher and a single mother. I was left a large inheritance by my uncle and I decided I'd like to bring up my children in more natural surroundings. I understand the property is close to the town of Gonvick and not far from a college in Crookston which would be fine for my boys. They're teenagers now and both of them want to pursue college degrees in environmental studies and hopefully get jobs with the Department of Natural Resources." She stopped, out of breath.

"I see, Mrs. Santa Anna. Yes, let me have Renee take your information and of course, we must do a criminal check. As soon as we have all that, I will call you and we can set up an appointment for you to visit me and see the property."

But W.D. was not interested in pursuing further conversation with her. He felt she was lying to him. No woman that had all that money and a job wanted to come to northern Minnesota to live. He doubted she had any children to bring up. He was pretty sure she was the secretary that the big shot was going to send to buy the property for him. Good luck with that. Renee got on the line and efficiently took down all the info she provided including her banking information.

"Time waster," he said as he relit his cigar. "I better get onto some of these other inquiries for the property. Here's an odd one from an attorney in Calgary. McNulty and Evensong calling on behalf of a client. Huh?" He looked over at Renee, " Ahhh and a man in St. Paul who says he's looking to build a summer home for him and his family."

"But, isn't there a house on the property already off the main road with a short driveway?"

"Yeah, guess he didn't read the ad…I think we've got a few prospective buyers now to check out. Are you ready?"

"Sure am. Do you want me to do the other two from California as well?"

"Oh, yeah, I guess so… although I probably know those results already. It's just one bid not two, from there."

W.D. took a big gulp of coffee from his cup with a wolf image on it. It crossed his mind to have his friend, Bureau of Criminal Apprehension Agent, Jon Andersen take a look into a few of these prospects. There was something just not right here. Ever since he'd found out that special piece of information while 'taking the opportunity' to glance through Washington Congressman Thayer Creswell's open valise over at his district office, he was suspicious of anybody who was interested in the land he had for sale. W.D. had no shame when it came to having document peeks or reading upside down when it was necessary. He hadn't even told Renee about what he'd found out and he wasn't going to. He would hold off for awhile because he knew she'd have a hard time handling it.

# # #

After supper at Shirley's Café in Fosston they decided to split up for the evening. Renee wanted to go home and check on the dogs and water the late blooming flowers and W.D. wanted to stay on in the office and catch up on a few things. He made a few calls after he checked his encyclopedia and his *Minnesota Atlas & Gazetteer*. He'd read only a few paragraphs, but he knew he had to go to the Cities as soon as possible. He thought about flying down there in his Cessna 180 Tail Dragger that he'd also purchased from the estate of Steve Olsen. He'd have to call his friend in Gonvick to see if he was free to pilot the Cessna.

Around 9:30 he tidied up the office and turned out the lights. He stood on the steps before he locked the door and looked out into the starry night. It was then that he heard it – the long shivery cry of the wolf – owoooooooooooo. He almost didn't breathe. Then he heard an answering howl. It sounded nearby. He mused about the distance their sound carried and guessed wolves kept in touch that way. He had seen a wolf only once and that was up near Ely on a hiking trip with the church group. That image had stayed in his mind: a silver-gray lightning-quick predator so beautiful in its powerful stance that it left an indelible memory. W.D. wished he could see a wolf again.

# # #

Two days later, after W.D.'s trip to St. Paul, it became clear that he'd better be loaded for bear. He'd become suspicious after reading Congressman Thayer's federal report but now it was confirmed by a friend in the state senate who had oil contacts that a new pipeline was urgently needed here in Minnesota. That meant the terminal in Clearbrook would have to be expanded or another built nearby. He was told that the property he owned in nearby Trail, situated like it was, next to state lands, would be valuable to a pipeline company. Instead of buying up hundreds of acres to go around these sensitive areas, they'd have a straight shot through his land. Now, how should he play this without divulging his knowledge of top secret-information? How could he force these buyers with the pipeline to reveal themselves?

He had land up for sale that he didn't want to sell to a pipeline company. His beautiful land, pristine and untouched, with clean water flowing through the Lost River, an environment that would be made toxic and corrupt from millions of gallons of oil gushing two to three feet below the surface, made him feel sick.

W.D. stayed in his office thinking about the land in Trail which was now his. He emptied out the last of the coffee from the pot and drank it down. He put his forehead down on the desk with his hands clasped into a pillow and reviewed the situation step by step: Land owners and farmers were in a depression worse than the one in the 1930's. Why? Well, he knew that the president's embargo on wheat to the Soviet Union was a huge factor. The decline in value of their land hit farmers hard. Some just sold for what they could get and headed for the Cities. Others rented to tenants. The rest welcomed the money from the pipeline companies whose easements were a way to stay in their homes and keep farming.

W.D. had heard the gossip about the right-of-way agent sitting at the kitchen table with the farmer and his wife negotiating a deal sometimes far below the real value of the land. He'd heard them say there were two constants in every landowner's easement sale. One was the value of land used for the right of way and secondly that the payment should compensate the landowner for any decrease in the overall value due to the damage they suffered from the construction and maintenance of a pipeline running through their property.

As a realtor, he'd tried to make good deals for the farmers and he often used the contract for deed as a flexible bill of sale. He always advertised farm sales in other states and sometimes in other countries to attract affluent buyers. He thought of the sale of the Barton lake home to the young television executive from New York City. Damn that was a good sale.

Now he faced the same threat as his clients, in the sense that a pipeline company would be soon, or already had, contacted him for an outright sale or an easement on his two valuable sections. He wondered if he could put the estate into a land trust?

Although eminent domain was not so common, he knew it wouldn't be long before it would become the norm. It was then that a frightful thought occurred to him. What if a pipeline company made an offer on his land and he refused it? He knew they had deep pockets. They were rolling in money. It occurred to him that Proctor Swinburne might be a straw buyer? Maybe for a pipeline company? What about that woman and her two sons? Those attorneys from Calgary? Who in the hell were they? Who did they represent?

He'd heard horror stories about the terrible plight

of farmers and landowners forced to sell their land to oil companies by eminent domain. He'd have to get some good advice. He sure didn't know how to play this game.

3

Just a few miles away, in McIntosh, Aunt Anita pulled her red Ford Escort into the parking space next to Gunhilde's mobile home. It was just a month before Halloween and the sisters were getting together to plan their annual candy and popcorn giveaway for the neighbor's children.

"Oh, good morning, Gunhilde, I see you've covered the hollyhocks." Aunt Anita stood beside the steps and perused the flower garden now in a state of disrepair due to an early frost.

"Come on in, Anita, I have some delicious poetica for brunch." Gunhilde untied her yellow apron as she reached up in the cupboard for the coffee cups. She let her Manx cat Maxwell out the door and he slowly crept around the edge of the trailer, careful not to seem too eager to climb the maple tree in the back of the property. The lower limbs were good for pouncing on rabbits or squirrels.

Aunt Anita hung her parka up on the birch wood hat rack and fluffed up her blonde hair.

"Have you heard from Dyanna lately?" Anita looked over at a studio portrait of her favorite – and only – niece. "It's awfully lonesome here now after she left."

"Well, it sure is," said Gunhilde, "but then I knew she could never make this area her home – it's too quiet. She needs her professional life."

"Hunh. I wouldn't call it quiet around here – a murder, a suicide, and a dozen break-ins – Los Angeles would be a relief," said Anita as she stared out the window. "How much different is it out there than here?"

"You know, I just don't know," said Gunhilde. Suddenly a glint came into her eye. "Say, let's go out there and check it out?"

"Oh yeah, I agree, Guny. Let's plan to go for Thanksgiving… maybe stay a month if Dyanna will have us."

Gunhilde thought for a bit. "You know, she just started her job. They had her on hold for six weeks."

"That is sure odd," said Anita. "Did they pay her to wait?"

"Huh, that is strange, too. She said they paid her salary and found a condo for her."

Aunt Anita sat down at the breakfast table and held out her cup for coffee. After Gunhilde poured, she took her pastry knife and cut two big slices of the honey-filled Slovenian dessert.

She heard some scratching on the outer door and got up. "I suppose its Maxwell."

But when Gunhilde opened the door she was surprised to see her neighbor, Harvey Swensen.

"Hi Gunhilde, say, I was wondering if I could borrow some coffee? Martha forgot to pick some up at the Super Six."

"Oh, sure you can. Come on in, Harvey." Gunhilde pulled out another chair for him and he eased into it. His eyes lit up when he noticed the poetica.

"Gosh, I'd sure like a slice of that. Martha says it's too much work to make." Harvey looked sad, "I have to drive over to Bemidji to get it from Raphael's Bakery."

"You bet you can," said Aunt Anita, as she cut a big piece for him. She felt sorry for the old guy.

After Harvey wiped the honey off his moustache, he looked at the sisters in mock seriousness. "Say, did you know that W.D. Caldwell and his wife Renee are going out to California?" He swallowed the last few crumbs and then started to divulge the surprising news. "I heard he got called by a television producer to help out on a documentary."

He got his breath and continued, "He paid W.D. a big wad of money in advance. I heard W.D. fed him a line about his investigative powers and even hoodwinked him so that he could bring his wife, too."

"I can't believe it," said Gunhilde.

"Well, I can," said Anita, "he's got some nerve. You know he told me to stop spreading the rumor that Dyanna's property was haunted. He's what the British call cheeky."

After another refill, Anita looked at Harvey and said, "Well, did you know Guny and I are going out to L.A., too? Maybe we'll run into them."

This was too much for Harvey and he slid his chair back, ready to go home. "Well, just lettin' you know he's going to be there, too. Hope that you really enjoy yourselves. Maybe you could give a talk at the McIntosh Senior Citizen's Center, you know, show some slides, when you get back."

"Oh yes, we'll do that, Harvey...let Maxwell in on your way out." She handed him a pound of coffee beans.

While the two sisters headed over to the telephone to call Dyanna, Maxwell jumped up on the table and had two big bites out of the poetica, cleaning his paws, before checking out his Friskies.

4

In an unusual twist of fate, W.D. Caldwell found himself owner of all of Olsen's property. He'd originally puchased the adjoining forty acre Kover property in an auction and had sold it back to Olsen just before he was killed. Now he owned the forty again plus the two sections of the Olsen estate.

He planned to keep the forty for himself and looked forward to rebuilding the log house and making repairs on the outbuildings. He'd design a place to relax and kick back without his family around. Kind of like a hunting cabin. He also wanted a small office, telephone, and Fax machine in case he had a deal go down. He'd already received quite a few inquiries and three bids on the Olsen sections and they were, to say the least, strange. He'd felt in his bones that anyone who wanted the Olsen estate probably had an ulterior motive and it would no doubt be criminal in nature due to the remoteness of the land. And he guessed, due to the infamy of Olsen's drug dealing activities that had gone on there.

He studied his sketches for the cabin and then picked up the telephone to call Maynard, his son-in-law, an expert in wood framing and trained carpenter, with a degree in construction from the local tech college.

"Good afternoon, Maynard, are you available for some carpentry and home repairs on the Kover log house?"

"Hi, Pops. Oh, yeah I am. You sure like that old place, don't you. Ahh, what's up? You need plumbing, hot water heater, air conditioner…?"

"Yeah, and a little more – I want patio carpeting installed in the kitchen, office, and hallways. When can you start, son?"

"Well, that depends. Do you still want me to work at night?"

"Nah, it's a daytime job now."

"Okay, can I hire the Charles boys to help me?"

"Yup."

"I can start tomorrow morning. Do you have a list of supplies needed?"

"Oh yes, all set to go. Use my credit card," he sighed. "You know it's strange to be out here without Olsen next door. I kind of miss those damn dogs, too."

"By the way, is it true they sold the dogs at the auction?"

"Yeah, they did. Moose Nelson bought them."

"Huh, that's funny. Wasn't he Lyneva's ex-husband?"

"Yeah, that's right."

"Say Pops, did you ever hear where Lyneva went after Olsen's murder?"

"No, I didn't. You know, she was kind of a weird chick. I checked out the house after I bought it and there wasn't a trace of her there. Steve's personal items were still all around, a pack of cigarettes, some playing cards, and a couple of books; but nothing of Lyneva's. It was as if she'd never lived there at all."

Although W.D. didn't mention it to Maynard, he knew from his insurance broker that Lyneva was the beneficiary of Olsen's big life insurance policy, doubled by his accidental death clause, which came to almost a million dollars.

Just then his office phone rang. "Son, I have to hang up." He turned to pick up his other telephone.

"Good afternoon, W.D. Caldwell Real Estate. If we don't have it – it don't exist. Oh, hi Renee." He listened intently.

"Oh, yeah, the guy from California – Proctor Swinburne?" He was suddenly alert. "When's he arriving?" He pulled out a ballpoint pen. "End of the week? Okay. Grand Forks International Airport? Oh sure, yes, and reserve a suite at the Grand Hotel in Crookston for him and his assistant. Uh huh, I guess so." He hesitated. "Nope, I'm going to stay out here tonight, hon." He smiled to himself. "Okay, see you. Good night, my dear."

# # #

W.D. leaned back in his recliner. It was mighty nice to be out here by himself. He had a few contracts to read, and then he planned to listen to the radio, to catch up on the news.

Around eleven, he got ready for bed. Before he settled in, he stepped outside to listen to the night sounds. He loved listening to the owl hoots, the frog chorus, and the wolf howls. It was very comforting to him. He went back inside the cabin, locked up, and switched off the lights, inside and out.

It was three in the morning, when W.D was awakened by the sounds of footsteps outside the cabin. His first thought was that it was a deer or a moose. But then he heard a man cough.

"What the hell?"

He swung his legs over the side of the bed, and reached for his pants, shirt, and glasses. He also felt for his Ruger handgun. He was never without it after his years with the BCA. He carefully stepped over to the back window and looked out onto the moonlit area around the shed. He saw a tall, middle-aged man looking around as if searching for something. This was extremely odd and looked like a threat. How had he gotten through the locked gate and the heavy pine stand?

What were his options? He could call out, "Who's there?" Or fire his pistol in the air over the guy's head? Or flick on the pole light near the shed and ID the person standing there. He decided on the last option. W.D. walked into the kitchen to the panel near the door and switched on the light pole. The light flashed through the log house as he turned around to see if he recognized his early morning caller.

No one was there.

My God, what have we got here? Was this a Big Foot disappearing act? He listened and then he heard the sound of a motor; an ATV was moving through the trees, out to the ditch on the main road, half a mile away.

How could a man move that fast? He thought for a bit. Yeah, he'd have to have an ATV close by. Ah huh, and someone to drive it.

He'd have Maynard make a tire mold from the pine stand and the road tomorrow and check for foot prints around the shed. He couldn't imagine why anyone would want to snoop around the Kover property. It had been posted for *No Trespassing* for almost a year. But more than that, it wasn't even up for sale.

5

The next day, W.D. returned to his office still puzzling over his late night visitor. "Oh, hon, the game warden has been calling you." Renee pulled out the telephone messages and handed them to W.D. After he filled his wolf cup with coffee, he sat down and returned the call.

"Hey, Duane, what's up, man? Find any gold out there in those wilderness creek beds?" W.D. sat back in his chair. He was glad to hear from his friend who was a long-time conservation officer.

"Ah no, W.D. just wonderin' what you got going over there at the Olsen place?" He sounded serious. Tried to get a hold of you last night. Been a couple of men staying there in Olsen's little house. Maybe came in the night before last? Lights are on in the house and there's a pickup truck and an ATV parked out front."

"Jeez! No, I don't have anything doin' out there. No one's allowed in there. I have a padlocked fenced gate on the driveway with a *No Trespassing* sign."

"Well, the gates open and the padlock was lying along the verge."

"God, guess I'd better get on over there right now. By the way, what were you doin' over there?"

"Checkin' on some traps over on the state land. But, listen W.D., you should call the sheriff and have him meet you out there." Duane was concerned.

"I'll call you back. Thanks, man. That's it – I'm on it." He hung up. "Damn it to hell."

# # #

About an hour later W.D. met Sheriff Roman Bahnrude and a deputy out at the property. The gate was still open but the men in the pickup were gone. They went through the house and it had a lived-in feeling. Meals had been prepared there and the bathrooms were in need of cleaning and deodorizing. Bahnrude had the door knobs and various spots dusted for fingerprints. He took photos and the deputy made some tire molds.

"You know, I had an interloper over on my property in the early morning hours. Big, middle-aged guy walking around. Disappeared in an ATV." W.D. felt like there was a connection. "We got some tire molds Maynard made that are coming back tomorrow."

"Good, we'll make a match with what we have. See any cig butts? DNA, you know."

"How long does it take to get the results?"

"Oh, sometimes a week or so."

There were no dishes, cups or glasses sitting around. Everything had been put in the dishwasher and washed up. W.D. was worried, "Could you send a deputy out here tonight to check the property?"

"Yup. But those guys won't be back." The sheriff helped W.D. put the gate up again and padlocked it.

W.D. knew the sheriff was right but he also knew this break-in meant trouble. He just didn't know how bad it was going to be.

6

It was exactly twelve noon on Friday when W.D. arrived at the Grand Forks International Airport. He was there to meet Mr. Swinburne, who'd supposedly arrived by private plane and would enter the airport from the FBO Entrance. Renee had made arrangements for him to stay at the Grand Hotel in Crookston along with a car rental: a large SUV with a licensed chauffeur as requested. W.D. planned to make two trips to the property. The first would be this afternoon when his leased helicopter would meet them at the Fosston Municipal Airport to fly them over the land for sale. The next day, they would drive to the property and walk it on foot to examine the streams, rivers, and building sites for the RV company.

His attention was distracted by a man aggressively pushing his way through the boarding passengers at the back of the airport. He thought that must be Swinburne. He was accompanied by two individuals; one looked like a security guard as he was wearing a holstered weapon, and the second, an assistant. As the man he figured was Swinburne headed for him, W.D. saw that he was in his fifties, fit and well built; wonderfully tailored in a dark brown blazer, Levis, white silk shirt and brown loafers. He stopped and looked carefully around and W.D. had a good look at his head. He had large features, a great haircut, suntanned swarthy skin, in an intelligent face. However as W.D, continued to stare, he became alarmed by the man's eyes: they appeared to be dark brown with thick black lashes.

"Greetings, you must be W.D. Caldwell?" The man's voice sounded like a professional broadcaster. "I'm Proctor Swinburne and I'm here to look at the property I'm buying in Trail."

W.D. was speechless as he continued to stare at the aggressive man who appeared to be wearing mascara on his eyelashes. One of Swinburne's two assistants, sensing his puzzlement, stepped forward.

"I'm Vernon Mattel, Mr. Swinburne's *aide de camp,* pilot, and VP of Operations, and I hope to make this two-day trip easy for Mr. Swinburne and that you come to terms over the prospective sale of the property in question."

W.D., although upset by the exchange, managed to say, "Glad you could make it, I have everything in place for your inspection." He indicated the hotel suites, the SUV rental, and chauffeur as requested.

As Mr. Swinburne came closer, he tried to shake hands with W.D., who backed away quickly and said, "Uh, Mr. Swinburne, we will not be able to make the trip by helicopter this afternoon as it does not accommodate more than two passengers."

He then handed Mattel a sheet with the details of their arrangements, "I can provide you with a telephone number of a flight company in the Cities that may be able to help."

"Thank you, W.D., we'll contact them, "said Mattel.

"No, we won't," said Swinburne. "We've already seen the land." He reached into his briefcase and brought out a large white envelope and handed it to W.D.

W.D. was surprised to hear this and while accompanying them to the departure exit of the airport and the waiting SUV, had a flash that they were the men who'd broken into his property. He nervously took the envelope, unsure what to do with it.

Swinburne appeared to be distracted. Mattel, on the other hand, was very relaxed and made small talk about this being their first visit to the northwest part of Minnesota and how exciting it was. He chatted easily about the high points of the region and had seemingly schooled himself on the statistics. "We'll go over to the hotel and freshen up, and then call you, W.D."

Mr. Swinburne said nothing.

"Okay, let's talk later." W.D. was very uneasy and eager to get away; quickly left and headed to the airport parking lot and his car. He headed back to his office in Erskine.

# # #

W.D. parked his Taurus near the back door of his office. He sat in it awhile thinking. He was concerned about what he just saw. It was not a scene he could immediately process, but he felt it was an attempt to intimidate him. Was it also an attempt to treat him as less than the professional he was? He slowly got out of his vehicle and entered the office deep in thought. He sat down at his big desk and felt relieved to be back on home ground. He put the coffee on and made a plan. First, he was going to call Swinburne and cancel any plans to show him the property. He was also going to tell him that it was not for sale. He looked up the number posted by Renee of prospective buyers. He dialed the number and was surprised when it was answered by a young lady.

"Good morning, this is the Pullman Committee, may I help you?"

"Uh, oh, I must have the wrong number. I was trying to reach Mr. Proctor Swinburne. I'm real sorry to bother you."

"Oh, no, please don't hang up; I can take a message for him. He's the owner of the company and currently out of town."

"Oh, well, my goodness. What kind of company is this? Where are you located?"

There was hesitation on the line. W.D. heard some papers shuffling. "This is Swinburne's RV Campground, Incorporated. May I help you?"

"Uh, yes, please give him this message from me – I'm W.D. Caldwell – that plans are cancelled to show him the property and it's not for sale at any price."

"I will give him the message, Mr. Caldwell. He calls in frequently."

"Thank you, ma'am."

He slammed the phone down and while his ire persisted he made another call to the Grand Hotel where Swinburne was staying. He left the same message with the hotel operator who said she would relay it immediately.

Next, he put in a call to Agent Jon Andersen at the Bureau of Criminal Apprehension in St Paul. As a former mercenary informant, W.D. enjoyed a good relationship with the Bureau and knew he could call them for information.

"Good afternoon. Say, I'd like to talk to Agent Andersen, this is W.D. Caldwell calling. Yes, that's right; I'm the one, hmmm, well, thank you. Okay, I can wait." W.D. poured himself a cup of coffee and sat back in his chair.

"Hey, Jon, good to hear your voice, yes, I guess so. Say,

I've got a problem I think you can help me with. Yeah, that's right. No, nothing illegal."

W.D. tried to succinctly convey his request: "I've got a client in from California named Proctor Swinburne who says he owns an RV Campgrounds and is interested in buying the Steve Olsen estate from me. Uh, Renee did a light background check on him before we proceeded to show the property. I need to know who he really is. Where does he live? What kind of business is he in? If he has any priors. Oh, yeah, I would appreciate that. The sooner the better. Yup, you too, son."

# # #

"Hey, W.D., got some news for you." It was a little after five in the afternoon and Jon Andersen was on the line.

"Hit me, son."

"Well, first of all Swinburne has numerous DUI's; but he has no other known priors. He's part of a family owned business called Environ-Oil in Oxnard, California. He branched off into a variety of business opportunities including a company in Las Vegas and one in St. Paul. He lives with his second wife and son on Mulholland Drive in Los Angeles. He owns several other homes: one in the Bahamas and one in London."

"Hmm, that's interesting. What's his net worth?"

"He's a billionaire, but he had an expensive and acrimonious divorce from his first wife, about a year ago, that's put him back some."

"What are the other two companies he owns?"

"The one in Las Vegas is a casino support company and the other in St. Paul is a pipeline company."

Andersen was cut off by a loud roar from W.D. "What? A pipeline company? My God!"

Jon continued with his narrative. "Uh, Proctor is 57 years old…."

"Say, does he have an RV Campgrounds?"

"No. No mention of anything like that."

"Yeah, no surprise there." W.D. was extremely annoyed. "I had a report of someone using the property for sale in the last couple of days and living in the house. They cut the padlock on the gate and drove a pickup in with an ATV."

"Hmm. Did you have the land posted?"

"Oh, yeah. I reported the trespassing and break-in to Sheriff Bahnrude."

"Say, W.D., I better do some more checking – this doesn't sound right. Weren't you going to show him the property? Isn't that why you met up today?"

"Yup. That's right. Huh, I'll never sell him that property now."

W.D. was pretty sure it was a land grab. Swinburne had plans to expand his pipeline company or some other devious boondoggle and decided to have a look around on his own terms without W.D.

"Oh, Jon, one last question. Why does a man wear mascara? I thought only women did that?"

"Ah, I don't know. Maybe he's gay? Or come to think of it – one of the agents here had glaucoma and the eye drops made his eyelashes grow."

"Well, no matter – I would never sell to him." W.D. was really angry and knew he needed time to cool down before he called the Grand Hotel to confront Swinburne.

"Thanks a lot, son," he started to unwind, "Your help is most appreciated. When are you coming up this way to visit?"

"Well, no plans at the moment. But, W.D., a word of warning, be careful – this could be a dangerous guy – trespassing on your property is a misdemeanor; a criminal act. I'll call you tomorrow. Talk to you soon. Call anytime, old buddy."

7

W.D. suddenly remembered the large white envelope given to him by Swinburne. It was not sealed and he opened it easily and read the contents. It was a signed Minnesota Purchase Agreement along with a check for $1,280,000.00 dollars to W.D. Caldwell from Swinburne's personal account. W.D. stared at the check. What the hell! Why that son of a bitch – he's laid a trap for me! I will never sign this. He decided then and there that he was going to drive over to the hotel and face Swinburne down. He picked up the phone and placed a call to his good friend Hans Derks, owner of the Grand Hotel.

"Good evening, may I speak to Mr. Derks, please? Yes, I'll hold on," W.D. switched hands so he could hear out of his good ear. "Okay, yes. Oh, Hans, this is W.D., oh yeah, okay, I guess, say, one of my clients checked in there earlier today – three suites, and I'd like to speak to Mr. Swinburne, please?" W.D. waited to be connected, but was surprised when Hans picked up again and said, "Oh, that party checked out early this afternoon."

"What? Really? Well, that was quick."

W.D. was then curious if they'd left any incriminating

material behind, "Hans don't clean the suites, I'm coming over right now – something's really weird here."

He slipped on his suede jacket, locked up and headed for his Taurus. It took him about half an hour to get over to Crookston and soon he pulled up in front of the hotel, put his Senior Parking Pass on the windshield, and headed for the front door.

Hans was waiting for him – still a handsome man in his old age, his white hair combed straight back and a predilection for wearing white shirts and a tie combined with a continental usage of *Vetivier* cologne, made him appear quite dapper.

"Why W.D. good to see you. I have the keys right here so we can go up and inspect the suite. Hmm, yes, mighty strange he left without contacting you."

W.D. also thought so and had an anxious feeling, especially after his meeting earlier with Swinburne who'd given him a signed purchase agreement and a whopper of a check – over a million dollars. They rode the elevator up to the second floor of the third story hotel. As they approached the first suite, the one Swinburne occupied, W.D. had a sense of doom.

But when Hans opened the door nothing was really amiss, several room service trays had not been picked up, the bedding was rumpled, and the pillows piled up for ease in sitting on the bed.

Next Hans opened the adjoining suite and it was clearly not used or occupied in any way. The sanitary paper banding was over the toilet seat and all was pristine: soaps not touched, water glasses unused, and the bed still had the coverlet in place. W.D. started to feel relieved. "Well, one more suite, isn't there?" He looked at Hans who said, "Yes, but that's across the hall." They left the two suites and stepped into the hallway.

Hans unlocked the door and they stopped in their tracks and stared disbelieving at the sight of a room – so trashed and bloodied that it just reeked of violence and pain. W.D. had seen only one other murder site and that was in East Grand Forks when Mrs. Bessie Barton shot Steve Olsen during a home invasion.

He was at a loss for words. He glanced into the bathroom stained with blood streaked walls and a rivulet of blood under the sink. He backed quickly out of the room, not wanting to touch anything. This scene called for the professional lawman.

"Let's get out of here, Hans," W.D. stepped out into the hallway. "Lock the doors and get any extra keys downstairs from the maids or room service and put them in your safe, do not touch the key pad of the door again." Hans followed W.D. down the hall where they quickly took the stairs down to his office.

As soon as they entered, Hans called the front desk to confiscate all keys for the three suites. He also ordered a carafe of strong black coffee and two cups. While Hans poured himself a double Scotch from his office bar, W.D. dialed Sheriff Roman Bahnrude, "Hey, Sheriff, its W.D. Caldwell here." He listened to the sheriff. "Ooh, not so good. Big time trouble here at the Grand Hotel. A bloodied bathroom in Suite #3. Yeah, we've secured the suites. No, we did not see a body. We'll be in Hans Derks's office. Yes, sir, I will." W.D. hung up.

He poured himself a bracing cup of black coffee and took a sip before searching for the number of the BCA. He found it and dialed, asking for Agent Jon Andersen, and adding that it was an emergency. Anderson picked up right away.

"Say, Jonny, its W.D. here, big time trouble, a bloodied bathroom here at the Grand Hotel. Yes, that one! I called you about him earlier today. No, did not see a victim. Oh, a Lincoln Town Car? Pronto." He hung up.

W.D. dug out a cigar from his suede jacket and fumbled around trying to light it. Hans, on the other hand, was on his third Scotch. "Jesus, I've never had a bloody mess like this in any of my hotels or motels – how will this impact on my business?"

W.D. slumped back in his chair and considered this. "Well, first of all, we didn't see a body – a victim – so hard to tell what went on." He hesitated. "I was reading <u>Hospitality Quarterly</u>, recently about a big New York hotel that actually had a gruesome murder in one of its rooms. Instead of disclosing the murder that occurred in there, they sealed the room after the investigation. Then they stripped it and turned it into a storage room."

"Oh, that won't work here in a small town – word will get out – you know that. Maybe there's some business in notoriety?"

"Huh, wouldn't count on it."

But W.D had an even bigger concern. He'd never agreed to any of the terms listed in the purchase agreement; only one he'd sign would be one he wrote. He also knew that the check had to be returned quickly and a reason given for it. He'd have to make a trip to the Cities to see his lawyer. He also planned to report Swinburne's strange behavior to Sheriff Bahnrude and to the BCA.

He asked Hans to call his contact at the airport to check on Swinburne's jet. He wanted to know when it arrived and how long it had been parked there. After waiting on the line for about five minutes, Hans immediately wrote down a telephone number, turned and looked over at W.D. questioningly, as he hung up the phone. He then called it and got additional information.

"No, he's gone. The jet departed today around 4:00 p.m. with a pilot and two passengers, headed for Las Vegas. It arrived four days ago, paid the tie-down fees, refueled, and was scheduled to depart today. Ah, here's the number of the company that owns the jet."

W.D. sat back in the chair to process the news. Why did Swinburne make an appointment with him and then look at the property without him? Why lay a purchase agreement on him and a big check and then leave town? Why was there a bloodied bathroom in one of the suites? Why was there no body? What was with Andersen's comment a few minutes earlier that it had been reported that several characters in a Lincoln Town Car had been picked up by Sheriff Bahnrude and questioned for acting suspicious near the Grand Hotel?

#   #   #

The next morning W.D. made an early morning call to his lawyers Harding & Nasset in Minneapolis. After explaining his situation, he was relieved to hear his lawyer Frank Nasset start laughing. "You know, W.D. you are the third client in the last two weeks that this stunt has been pulled on."

"What the hell? What's going on Frank?" W.D. was beside himself with a rising anger.

"Nothing that we can't fix for you in a jiffy. Send the purchase agreement and the check over to us by Federal Express and we will terminate this crock outside of the court room in a couple of days."

"My God. Really glad to hear that. What's the story?"

"Pipeline companies trying to get a leg up on buying land for a new pipeline or terminal. They've got so much money they'd stop at nothing to make a deal. Ah, Swinburne may have only needed 400 acres, but he could have eventually used the rest of the land as a buffer or extra acreage to sell."

"I must admit, I never got a check that big before." W.D. smiled.

"But they got tangled up with the wrong guy when they took you on." Frank had a long association with W.D. and knew how tough he was. He knew the old dude didn't back down.

"Well, mighty glad we can nip this in the bud, Frank. Hope you can make it up this summer so we can do some fishing."

"Yup, you betcha. I'll get on this as soon as I receive the paperwork. Best to Renee."

All was right again in W.D.'s world. At least for the moment. He sat back in his chair, enjoying the quiet of the office.

W.D. was pleased by the termination of the purchase agreement with Swinburne and the return of the check. But he doubted that it was the end of his troubles with the California tycoon.

8

It was late in the afternoon and W.D. was finishing off some work on a contract in his office. He thought he heard a knock on the screen door. He listened a bit and again heard a soft rap.

"Come on in," said W.D. although he couldn't actually see anyone. He stood up as the door opened and a little boy stepped shyly inside.

"Well, well, what can I do for you, son?" W.D. could not see anyone else behind him. "Is your mama with you?"

"Ah, hello, Mr. W.D., No, she's not…my name is Lancelot Myron Haskins, I live over behind the gas station," he stopped. He stood quietly for a moment and then burst out: "I'd like to work for you. I could help out here like I do at home for Mama." His blue eyes were filled with sincerity and an underlying sweetness.

W.D. was taken aback. He had never seen this little boy before. He did not know his mother but knew she worked nights at the local hospital. She was the widow of Myron Haskins, who had been accidentally killed in 1986 while excavating a pipeline trench in northern Minnesota. Lance's grandfather Hank Haskins worked over at the Crookston Courthouse.

"Why, how old are you, son?"

"I'm going to be ten years old…next year, sir."

"Kind of anxious to go to work, aren't you?" He smiled as he thought of how different he was from most boys his age. A thought occurred to him; he mulled it over, and came to a conclusion. "Why yes, I just might have a job for you. Ah, I think you could help me." He looked around for his humidor, reached in and plucked out a cigar, and lit it.

The little boy was fascinated by this maneuver. He did not know anyone who smoked and he wondered at this secret ceremony. He stared at the faint trail of cigar smoke wending its way to the ceiling, then spreading out like an evening fog.

W.D. started to make his offer, planning as he went: "I could hire you, Lance, for an hour every night starting at five in the afternoon – you know after your classes were over – for, say, $7.00 a week in wages to start and then pay for your supper, too, five nights a week at Shirley's Café."

W.D. thought some more.

"Your job will be to empty wastebaskets into trash bags, take them to the dumpster down the block, wash out the coffee pot, clean the glass panes in the door as well as the door knobs, and sweep up the office floor. How does that sound, son?"

"Oh, Mr. W.D. I'm so happy. Yes sir, I know I can do just exactly that and more." He pushed his dark red hair back off his forehead and said almost as an afterthought: "Do you want me to get started now?"

"Well, no, let your mama know. You can start tomorrow night if she approves." He walked around his desk and over to the little boy, holding out his hand. "It's a deal, son."

Lance reached out and W.D. took his soft little palm into his and they gently shook on it.

\# \# \#

In the first few weeks, W.D found it disconcerting to be called Mr. W.D. He wondered why he wasn't called Mr. Caldwell. He also was startled by the continuous use of sir, a respectful term used mostly by Southerners. One afternoon he happened to take a closer look at Lance and realized that his front teeth had not grown in completely and the name Mr. Caldwell came out Mr. Cudwell. He called Renee Mrs. W. without the D and she accepted this without comment. In fact, she was charmed by the little boy and impressed by his ability to clean and stick to his duties.

The hiring of Lance had worked out just fine for everybody. W.D. had been visited by Lance's mother, Twilah, who thanked him for hiring her son. She usually worked until eleven and now she didn't worry as much about her boy because he made sure he got home before dark. W.D. also got a letter from his friend Haskins over at the courthouse, thanking him for being a role model for his grandson, and inviting him to coffee anytime he was in Crookston.

W.D. always stopped to chat with Lance. How was school going? What was he studying? W.D also encouraged Lance to give him reports about what he saw around town, no matter how insignificant. Lance enjoyed this and started his work day with an update of what neighbors he'd run into, what he was doing in school, and what he planned for the weekend.

\# \# \#

After two months on the job, Lance had a longer report than usual: "Mr. W.D. I was in Shirley's last night for supper and two funny men came in."

"What do you mean, son…funny?"

"Well, they were really big and one was fat and they smelled like you."

W.D. looked at Lance in surprise: "Why, what do you mean, boy?"

"They smelled like cigar smoke, sir. They'd parked their big, black car out front and it had funny dark windows. They sat in a booth near me and ordered something strange. Mot-zaa ball soup – well, that's what it sounded like."

W.D. didn't know what that was. He looked around for his dictionary. After a lot of false tries he found Matzo Ball Soup, a traditional Jewish dumpling in a broth.

"What did Ms. Shirley say to that?"

"She said all she had was potato soup and – and they said they'd take that instead."

"Hmmm."

"I thought it was funny that they had on white shirts and neckties like our preacher wears. But they swore a lot and I don't think they were ministers, do you?"

"No, Lance, I don't think so."

W.D. was impressed by Lance's observation and detail of description. He wondered who these men were. He wondered if they were still around. Dark windows? Humph, sounded pretty sneaky. He thought of the car mentioned by Jon Andersen as being suspicious around the Grand Hotel.

The next day he saw a black Lincoln Town Car glide slowly past Caldwell Realty. He would soon understand why these men were in Erskine and he wouldn't like it one bit.

9

Lance Haskins felt happier than he'd been in a long time. He thought about that old feeling he used to get in the pit of his stomach when he left school in the afternoon. He would be so lonesome; he had nothing to look forward to. After errands and his school work, he would watch PBS until ten. Mama worked until eleven at night and he was usually asleep when she came in.

Now after two weeks everything had changed. He'd found a job. A job where he was needed, a job where he fit in. He looked forward to catching up with Mr. W.D. when he got to work. He was always waiting for him with a glass of milk and he'd let him know how many properties had come in – how many acres they had, how many buildings. Then Lance would tell W.D. about school, his subjects, how he'd raised his hand when he knew the answer, what he ate for lunch, the games he played, and sometimes the tricks Lonajean pulled on him.

Today, he changed his tee shirt and grabbed a bulky woolen sweater to wear when he walked home this evening. He carefully checked the house and locked the front door. He decided to walk along Cameron Lake in Friar's Park because he was early for work. He loved the park; it had been his playground ever since he and Mama moved to Erskine after Papa died. He stepped up on the elevated landing that led directly to the beach and then took a left veering off onto the grass until he reached the sidewalk. He could see the sun was starting to go down but it still had that burst of last brilliance.

He took out his new yo-yo; it was a gift from Lonajean. It was made of wood and had a Danish design on the side. It had belonged to her brother, who was now in high school. He smiled when he thought of Lonajean. She was not a scaredy cat like some girls. She'd made friends with him right away when he'd started the second grade in Erskine. He remembered how frightened he was and how he just wanted to hide somewhere. He wouldn't look at anyone. She sat in the desk behind him and got acquainted by tickling his neck with a long blade of grass. She made him laugh and soon he was pulling her braids in retaliation. Now they were in fourth grade and always ate lunch together sometimes trading sandwiches.

Lance was really getting the hang of how the yo-yo worked. He'd throw it horizontally and it propelled itself out about a foot or so. He was thrilled and rather surprised. Then he moved it vertically and it responded. He was so immersed in the yo-yo that he didn't see a black Town Car glide by and then slow down. It stopped and waited for Lance to catch up. Lance looked over and saw the car, recognized it as the same one outside Shirley's Café, with the dark windows. He knew who was in it: the two men, dressed like ministers. He stopped playing with the yo-yo and stared at them. Then the car window rolled down: "Say, little man, could you direct us to the Caldwell Realty Office?"

A heavyset man with a short neck and bald spot in the

back swiveled his head to look at Lance.

"Oh, yes, sir. Uh, take a left on Main Street and then make a right on Harvest Road. It's about a quarter of a mile and it's a log cabin office with a big sign." Lance felt relieved that he could help these men. They were kind of strange acting and he had his guard up. His mama had given him the age-old warnings of do not take candy from strangers or accept any rides.

"Well, thanks sonny, you are certainly a smart little boy. Why don't you step over here so I can give you a dollar for your help?"

"Uh, no thank you sir, but I don't need any money."

The fat man seemed not to hear him as he proceeded to slide out of the car, grasping the door for support to stand up. He seemingly made an effort to pull a wallet out of his back pocket; but instead pulled out a white handkerchief wrapped in cellophane.

He stepped forward to where Lance was standing, and grabbed him with his left hand, shoving the handkerchief in his face with the right. Lance choked and started to scream for help and squirmed to get out of his grip. The last thing he saw was a second man coming toward him. He realized there was a strong odor on the handkerchief and felt as if he was going to black out. He fell to the sidewalk unconscious.

#   #   #

"Okay now Max, you old *klutz*, what the hell are you going to do with him?" The other fellow, quite a bit younger, and many pounds lighter, glared at the man holding Lance's small frame.

"Sheldon, you know we had to make a move…had to make an effort. The Boss insisted and you know how he is." He took the chloroformed handkerchief away from Lance's face and shook it out, returning it to the cellophane bag, "now help me here, please."

"Yeah, you know I will," said Sheldon disgustedly. "So let's tie his hands, then carry him to the car and lay him in the back seat, before someone comes by."

They hurriedly put Lance in the back seat and covered him with a pink and purple afghan. They both got back in the front seat, actually shocked that not a single person had come by. Max started the car, sweat running down into his eyes and dripping onto the steering wheel. They slowly glided away.

"Do you have a single plan in your head, you old *shlimazel?*"

Max was at a loss for an idea. "Well, I suppose we have to take him back to our cabin in Maple Lake."

They'd rented a large cabin for the month and it had a good deal of privacy. It was right on the lake and they had the use of the small launch that came with the cabin.

"Uh hum. Yeah and then we have to arrange for his meals, we have to put him in my bedroom because it's clean and the windows lock, and we have to talk to him—he's going to cry—we need to reassure him, that we have only kidnapped him for a few days so his Grandpa Caldwell will come to terms on the sale of that land in Trail that the Boss wants. That it's like ransom to get him back."

Max looked at Sheldon with admiration.

"*Mazel Tov!* I knew you'd come through." He looked over his shoulder into the back seat where Lance was still asleep. He felt bad doing this but then again, maybe they could make it fun for the little boy. Take him out in the boat and do some fishing. As they headed for Highway 2 and the four miles to their cabin, he realized that he never seriously thought they would ever pull off the kidnapping of this little boy. But it had been so easy.

"Max, stop at McDonalds in Mentor, I want to buy him half a dozen burgers and fries, and a case of Coke. Also some chocolate chip cookies and a few quarts of milk."

"How about something for me, too." Max pulled out his cigar, but he was too nervous to smoke it.

"I planned to get us some takeout from the Casino – I've already called it in. Just have to pick it up it up a little later," said Sheldon as he grabbed the cigar away from Max and stuck it in the glove compartment. "You are such a *gornisht*."

#   #   #

It was after 6:30 when W.D. finished with a new contract for the Severson Farm. He looked over at the milk he'd poured out for Lance and was shocked by the realization that Lance was not in the office. He had not arrived for work. At first he thought maybe a ball game or a class project had delayed him. No, Lance was not the kind of boy who would do that. He would call the office. He sat back down behind his desk and wondered what to do. Renee had left at five to meet some friends from the Augustana Ladies Aid so he couldn't consult her. He called Lance's home, but there was no answer. Then he decided to call Mrs. Haskins at the hospital where she was the night nurse. She would know where he was.

"Good evening, may I speak to Mrs. Twilah Haskins, please?"

The switchboard receptionist said, "Oh, of course, may I tell her who is calling?"

"Yes, ma'am, it's W.D. Caldwell."

"Oh, just one moment, W.D." She came back on the line, "Just one moment... you're lucky because she's on her break." He heard the connection as Mrs. Haskins picked up the extension.

"Good Evening it's Twilah Haskins, may I help you?"

"Yes ma'am, I'm sure you can help me. Lance did not show up for work tonight and I hoped you could tell me what come up to deter him from his job?"

"What-t-t-t? Lance did not show up for work? My God. Something is awfully wrong. Mr. Caldwell, you have to call the Sheriff right away. My little boy is so careful – he'd never do that." She started to moan and seemed to try and stop herself from crying in jagged spurts. "Oh Mr. Caldwell, don't let any time go by in the search for my son!" W.D. heard the phone drop and a lot of noise at the other end. He decided to hang up, too. Then he put in a call to Sheriff Roman Bahnrude.

# # #

"Good evening, Sheriff Bahnrude, this here's W.D. calling you with some bad news – we've lost a little boy over here in Erskine!"

"Well, hello there W.D...ah, just slow down a bit here and let's get a report." Bahnrude was used to getting a missing child report as he got one at least once a month. Usually they played hooky or stopped over at a friend's house and forgot to call home. But he knew that W.D. understood law enforcement and would not make a call unless he felt it was urgent.

"What is the full name and address of the child? Age? And circumstance?"

"It's Lance Haskins of Erskine. He lives with his mother Twilah on Greer Avenue. He's almost 10 years old and was expected at my office around 5:00 p.m. where he has a part-time job emptying waste baskets and tidying up. I hired the little guy about a month ago and he spends an hour or so here and then I send him to Shirley's Café on my tab for his supper. He's as reliable as they come and when he didn't show up I called his mother over at the hospital where she works and – well – she got hysterical."

"It's after seven now so let's do some routine checking before we move this to the next step. Can you call up his friends – get their names from his mother, call the school, his teacher or the principal, see if they have any ideas, and check with Shirley at the café. Did he have his supper there tonight? Get back to me with a report. Hmm, I will have to call this into the BCA, maybe get an agent up here to help out on this."

Around nine, W.D. called the sheriff. "Well, nothing to report, nobody seen him after school and he didn't show up at Shirley's Café tonight. I called a few of his relatives, too, just in case he decided to visit, and they haven't seen him either."

"Uh, W.D. you know, we have to have some evidence that he was abducted. Any ideas?"

"No, I can't say I do right now. I think I'm going to stay in the office tonight in case there's a break in the case. Thanks, Roman, keep me updated. I sure feel awful bad about this – I think a lot of that little boy."

"Yeah, I know, and we'll do all we can and then some to get him back home to his mother," said the sheriff, "if you get any ideas, give the station a call and tell the dispatcher. They'll get in touch with me."

10

"That poor little *goy*. He cried all night." Max was beside himself with concern for little Lance. They were on their way to Grand Forks, a city of over 50,000 people, just over the Minnesota-North Dakota border, to see their boss's lawyer.

"Well, I guess he's really scared. Who wouldn't be?" Sheldon glared at Max who was driving. "I just hate it when we have to do this kind of thing. *Feh!*" Sheldon put his hands over his eyes. "Kidnapping is serious. It's a felony. How many years would we get?"

"Maybe ten or more in Stillwater. Ohhhh. Now I feel so bad. I've been there you know. Its maximum detention." He almost went off the road. "Umnn what did you tell him this morning to make him stop screaming?"

"I said he'd only be with us for a day or two and then we would take him home to his mama," Sheldon looked pained. "I also said we were hiring him to help us clean the cabin before we left. Then I went on to explain what we wanted done: first clean the bathroom, then vacuum the rugs, and then do a load of laundry." Sheldon continued. "Then, I said he could watch TV– I locked all doors and windows."

Max looked shocked. "You what? You put him to work?"

"Uh huh, uh, he's got good sense and realizes there is a

reason behind his captivity."

"Are you saying you want him to stay busy so he doesn't panic?"

"No, I want him to feel part of this adventure."

"*Oy Vey*. You are such a *schmooze!*" Max shook his head in disbelief.

"I think we should buy him a bicycle in Grand Forks. A red one." Sheldon closed one eye and looked over at Max, "and then a little puppy, too."

"Max's face lit up. "Do you think that would be *kosher*? I mean I'm all for it. I never had one and felt so bad that my folks were too poor to buy me one."

"Oh, so that's why you fell into a life of crime. Stealing all the things your folks couldn't buy you?" Sheldon scratched his head, "you know, I did have a bike and riding it around my neighborhood was some of the happiest times of my life."

"Say, where are we going?" Max looked blank. "Oh, now I remember. Sniderman & Son."

"Yeah, Sniderman or as I like to call him – Spiderman. That old goof. You know there is no son, don't you?"

"No, I didn't know that. Hmmm, we're supposed to pick up a purchase agreement for W.D. to sign and a ransom note for his grandson."

Max slowed down as they approached the Columbia Mall. "Hey, let's stop at Bagel's Plus and get some lunch."

"Sounds good to me. This is probably the only bagel place within a hundred miles of Maple Lake."

After finishing off four bagels apiece, brushing crumbs off their shirts, rubbing a napkin across their thick lips, they felt renewed, and headed out for Sniderman & Son.

Max pulled the Town Car up to the front of the office building that had a billboard that stated "You Have Reached

Sniderman & Son. Our Team of Lawyers Can Handle All Your Legal Problems in One Stop."

Sniderman was standing on the front steps watching as they parked the big car. "Come on up, boys, everything is ready for you."

"Hello Sam, good to see you again." They got out of the car, stretched and waddled over to the steps. They trundled up making little groans and finally stepped into the big game room-like office. A giant moose head welcomed them, next to that were two female deer heads, and then an indescribable animal – a beaver or a porcupine – the boys didn't know what it was. Max sat down on a picnic bench while Sheldon perched on a low coffee table. They wondered what kind of place this was that had no sofa. They stared at Sam who'd ensconced himself behind a big maple desk.

"I want to go over Proctor's instructions again. I want to make sure you understand them," droned Sam. "First thing, drop the ransom note and contract already signed by Proctor at Caldwell's door tonight. Attach this note with instruction that he is to bring the $20,000 in hundreds and the signed contract to St Luke's Cemetery just outside McIntosh by five tomorrow afternoon. The $20,000 is for you and Sheldon to split. The contract, with Caldwell's signature, is to be returned to me at once."

"Oy, we'll bring it back ASAP," said Max.

They turned to leave. "Who would have thought you were the great white hunter," said Sheldon as he looked disapprovingly at a paper weight with a bird wing on it.

"Oh, I'm not," said Sam, "a taxidermist client owed me money and I took these trophies as payment."

"Huh. Well, see you again soon."

They left the office carrying a large white envelope

with an image of two crows across the front and the words, 'URGENT FOR W.D. CALDWELL' handwritten with a black marker pen. Sheldon wondered about the crow image. He thought they might be an ill omen.

"He is one creepy dude," said Sheldon. "I wonder what else he takes as payment for his services."

# # #

As they pulled away from the curb they spied a pet shop in the next block. "Let's go get that little puppy for Lance," said Max.

"Good idea," said Sheldon, "wonder what kind of puppies they have?"

They drove to the next block and parked right in front. There was a little puppy in the window and it looked at them with interest.

"Oh, is he ever cute. Wonder what kind of dog that is?" Max got out of the car and stood in front of the window. Then he turned and led the way into the shop, Sheldon close behind him. They stopped once inside and looked around. The owner seeing their hesitancy rushed up to them to ask if he could help them.

"Uh, maybe," said Sheldon as he bit on a tooth pick, "how much for the kittens?"

"Well, I can sell them all for $45…they've got their shots and they're almost half-Persian."

"Huh. Nah, I don't think so. How much is the puppy in the window?"

"Well, he's a top of the line yellow lab, about 6 weeks old, his mother was grand champion in the Fargo dog show last year, but his father is a nobody. We are asking $700 and that's a giveaway price," said the owner with a suspicious look at Sheldon, "why are you interested in him?"

"Oh, our grandson wants a dog," volunteered Max, "and he looks like a nice puppy – but we don't want to spend that much."

The store owner looked thoughtful, "No, I really can't sell him for one penny less, sir." He was having qualms about selling the puppy at all and thought he might up the price to discourage them.

"I was offered $800 for him from a buyer from Fargo who knows his linage, uh, so you see then that's it…"

"Well, if we pay that, what about throwing in a year's worth of dog food gratis?"

After twenty minutes of squabbling, they agreed on $750 plus six months of free dry food and 20 percent off on a dog kennel. Sheldon then turned around and bought $200 worth of dog toys at regular price.

"We're parked out front – the big Town Car – could you give us a hand with the dog carrier and all the dog toys?" Sheldon suddenly realized that they might have a little dog crying in the back seat, "say, how much for the dog blanket to put over the carrier?

"Oh, ah, that's a gift from me."

Max pulled out his wallet and counted off a $1000 dollars and a $20 tip to the owner.

The shop owner got the blanket down from the display wall, carried it out to the car, along with the kennel with the puppy in it. He set the kennel down in the seat and draped the blanket over it. He looked over at the two sweaty men in amazement. Just what kind of men were they, anyway? Even though he'd made profit today, he suddenly felt sorry for the little puppy.

#   #   #

Once settled in the car, they took off slowly, and Max sighed, "what a cute little *boychik* – I never had a puppy. Did you, Sheldon?"

"Oh yeah, I had three or four little puppies, oh, not at one time, but they made me so happy, they slept with me at night. They became one of the family."

"Oh, Lance is going to be so happy. I can't wait to see his face when he sees the puppy. And the bike."

"Oh Gawd, the bike! We forgot to get it."

"Let's stop at Kmart on Highway 2."

They pulled into the Kmart parking lot and wasted no time in buying a red bicycle with a one year warranty and a searchlight for night riding. The clerk took it off the display floor, and transported it out to their car, and expertly tied it onto the roof. They charged the bike to Sheldon's credit card and Max gave the clerk a $20 tip. It all took less than twenty minutes.

The big Town Car bounced along – headed for Maple Lake – a bicycle tied to the roof and a puppy in a kennel on the back seat, dry dog food and toys stuffed into plastic bags, filling up most of the floor space.

In the front seat, Sheldon stared down at the big white envelope with the crow images. He wondered if they were two *mishegas* and not for the first time.

11

A large, golden moon slipped out from behind a cloud briefly illuminating the small village of Erskine. It cast a glow into the darkened office window of W.D. Caldwell Realty revealing a man with a telephone receiver in his hand and his body bent into a collapsed position. It was W.D and he was on his second all-nighter and he looked as bad as he felt. He'd had a terrible day; his efforts had been so futile, there was no trace of little Lance, no one had seen him since he left school the day before.

W.D. straightened up, looked out at the moon, and realized that not only had he hit a dead end in his search: he was also starving. He'd had no supper and now it was midnight. He thought he'd better make an effort to relax. He hung up his jacket, had a quick wash, and headed for the small lunchroom where he kept an array of pizzas, popcorn, sodas, and milk. He put a small Tony's Pizza in the microwave and opened a Coke. He had a bowl of apples on top of the fridge and he took one for dessert.

After finishing his meal, he cleaned up and decided it was time for a nap in his oversized recliner. He got his favorite Bemidji Woolen Mills blanket out from one of the file cabinets and settled down. All the lights were off except the one on the back porch. He instantly dozed off. But he woke up with a start when he heard a dull scratching noise on the front door of the office. Was somebody trying to break in?

He didn't move; listening attentively. Soon he heard steps on the front porch. He got up slowly and clumsily felt his way over to a window where he could see the parking lot. A tall man was just getting into a Lincoln Town Car illuminated by the interior lights, but due to the darkened windows he was not recognizable. The car started up, and rolled out of the parking lot and onto the street, the tail lights visible until it turned left onto the highway.

He quickly went to the front door, opened it, and saw a large white envelope taped to the door. He switched on the porch lights and saw that the envelope had an image of two crows along with a hand-written salutation 'URGENT FOR W.D. CALDWELL' on the front. W.D. stood there staring at the envelope, wondering what to do next. After careful consideration he decided he had to find a pair of gloves so his fingerprints wouldn't be on the envelope and then secondly he had to find his Polaroid Camera to take pictures before he removed it. Then he had to call Sheriff Bahnrude to get over here in case it was a ransom request.

After slipping on the gloves, he removed the envelope from the door; carried it inside to his desk, slit it open with a sharp paper cutter, and removed two items: a Purchase Agreement between W.D. Caldwell Realty and the Pullman Committee Entertainment Group in Las Vegas, Nevada; the second was a ransom note.

He spread it out and examined it:

WE'VE GOT YOUR GRANDSON LANCE HASKINS AND HE IS SAFE. FOR NOW. SIGN THE ENCLOSED CONTRACT AND PAY $20,000

IN $100 BILLS IN RANSOM FOR HIS RETURN. BRING SIGNED CONTRACT AND MONEY IN A BLACK GARBAGE BAG AND PLACE ON THE GRAVE MARKER FOR CONNALLY IN ST LUKES CEMETERY IN MCINTOSH BY 5 PM TOMORROW. THE CROWS.

W.D. was shocked to find out that they thought that Lance was his grandson. He was also shocked by the purchase agreement as it was for the estate of the late Steve Olsen. Many people had inquired about buying it. Only one person had shown up to view it. Only one person had exhibited strange and suspicious behavior who wanted to buy it. Only one person had the guts to kidnap a child and run a deal like this: R. Proctor Swinburne. He knew why, too. Swinburne planned to run a pipeline through his property at any cost.

It was two in the morning, but he put in a call to dispatch at the Crookston Sheriff's office.

"Say, I wonder if you could contact the Sheriff. Huh? Well this is W.D. Caldwell and I've been contacted by the kidnappers of Lance Haskins. Ah, with a ransom note. Yeah, two men stopped by after midnight. Okay. Tell him to get over to my office. Pronto. Ah huh. Yeah. Thanks."

Half an hour later a squad car, brakes squealing, slid into the parking lot of the Caldwell Realty. It was Roman Bahnrude and his newly appointed driver, Deputy Hans Tollefson, of Bemidji Speedway fame. They quickly got out of the car and entered the office. W.D. had coffee ready and put out two mugs with a jug of milk and a bowl of sugar. He had the ransom note and the contract for deed spread out on his desk held down by a loon paperweight.

"Say, I'm sorry, Sheriff, I took that note off the door before you got here. Ah, I didn't know what we were dealing with –

anyway I used gloves and I have taken pictures." W.D. wiped his eyes. "Damn, it's worse than I ever thought it could be."

He proceeded to tell the sheriff about Proctor Swinburne while the sheriff examined the note and the contract. "Hmm, yeah, this looks mighty bad. I'm going out to the squad car to use the phone to call the BCA for help." He turned to go back outside but W.D. stopped him.

"Oh, umm, Sheriff, I have a special request to make of the agent – it's pretty unconventional – know what I mean?"

"Well, no, I don't, W.D., but sure, come on; you're well connected to them – being an informant for so long."

The sheriff phoned in his request for help. Finally he was patched through to Agent Jon Andersen; he'd been contacted while on surveillance duty. W.D. talked softly to him for about five minutes.

"Okay then, let's go get 'em," W.D. signed off. "See you in the morning."

But the sheriff was not done. He used his radio system to call in an APB.

"This is an all-points bulletin from Sheriff Roman Bahnrude. Be on the lookout for a black Lincoln Town Car with dark windows, plates not known, driver and passenger wanted for questioning in the kidnap of a child from Erskine. Apprehend and bring in to the nearest police station; considered armed and dangerous. Over and out."

# # #

Around 8:30 in the morning W.D. pulled into the parking lot of the First National Bank in Fosston. He was there to get the ransom money for Lance. After talking with Brandon Berkquist the bank president, he sat down and waited while the head cashier arranged the $20,000 in labeled packets of $100 bills. He'd taken $10,000 from his checking account and $10,000 from his business account as per federal compliance. Although W.D. had watched TV shows where bad guys requested unmarked bills, he thought it did not exist. Berkquist confirmed this by telling him that banks do not scan or record serial numbers of incoming cash and neither does the Federal Reserve Bank. The money was arranged neatly in a briefcase provided by the bank. W.D. picked it up, surprised by how light it was; and after thanking everyone profusely, strode out to his car, and returned to Erskine.

Renee was in the office and had taken charge – the blanket was folded up, the floors vacuumed, and everything was put back in working order. She was busy answering the many calls that were coming in concerning Lance. Many people in Erskine had heard the APB about his kidnapping on their scanners and the town was abuzz with the news; horrified that an innocent young boy had been snatched in the daytime, and downtown at that.

"Oh, W.D. I'm so glad you're back," said Renee, "these phone calls are almost too much for me to handle – by the way, one came in from Shirley at the Café, and she really wants to talk to you. She thinks she may have a description of the kidnappers."

12

Agent Jon Andersen circled the Fosston Municipal Airport in his Cessna 152 and then radioed his final approach to land on runway 34 to other planes in the area. He was glad Agent Emil Nelson of Bemidji would be assisting him. The kidnapping of young Lance Haskins might end tragically if not played right. The BCA Agent was surprised by the purchase agreement request for signature and the necessity for W.D. to sign before Lance was returned. The ransom money cited seemed an afterthought and was really an insignificant amount as far as such demands went.

Emil was standing at the gate waiting while Andersen tied down the plane. "You sure got a hell of a case here, my friend," he said as he shook Andersen's hand. "Hey, it's good to see you, again."

Less than an hour or so, they arrived at Caldwell Realty. W.D. jumped up to greet the agents.

"God…so good to see you guys, come on in, and get some coffee." He sat down again. "I have Shirley over at the Café on the line, she just heard that they've spotted a black Town Car headed for Grand Forks. She has a description of them!"

Andersen pulled up a chair and sat down, while Emil

poured out two cups of W.D.'s famous coffee made with beans ordered directly from Colombia.

"Jeez, W.D.'s got a description of the kidnappers." Andersen was filled with admiration for W.D. "and now's he's got a tail on the car." He started to laugh and shake his head even though he was extremely concerned about the case. Emil looked over at W.D. and just shrugged.

As soon as he hung up the telephone, W.D turned to Andersen and said, "Son, did you get that ink I asked for?"

"Oh, yeah, I've got it right here." Andersen took out a small package and unwrapped it. "I tried it out before I left Burt's Magic Shoppe and Burt himself has personally timed its legibility before it becomes fugitive."

"Well, how long is that?" W.D. was intently staring at Andersen.

"Ah, around ten hours."

"Huh, better get this thing signed right now," said W.D., "and hope to hell it works like it's supposed to."

Both agents were anxious to get a look at the contract and the ransom note. Andersen read them both and thought of how to apprehend the person who picked up the black bag. It was one weird note. A cemetery?

"The purchase agreement is an executable contract with my signature," said W.D., "but we know it's not going to last."

"This ink is a stroke of genius," said Andersen, "but what about the money?"

"Oh, I have it here in packets of $100 bills."

"W.D., you are damn amazing," said Emil. "What's left for us to do?"

"Well, let's discuss the apprehension at the cemetery," W.D. looked from one to the other, "but first let me give you the description of the alleged kidnappers." He proceeded to give details of the two men and their car.

"We think it's best to drop the black garbage bag around 4:30," said Andersen, "say, are you familiar with that McIntosh Cemetery?"

"Oh, sure am and I know where Samuel Connally's grave is located. He had a lot to do with building the railroad through Polk County," said W.D.

"Is there enough room for one or both of us to hide back of the stone monument?"

W.D. thought for a moment and then said, "There's heavy shrubbery near the stone that would be easy to approach through the woods back of the graveyard."

"Okay, so W.D., let's get that contract signed, get the briefcase with the cash, and pack it all up in the black garbage bag, and head out to the cemetery."

Anderson looked at Emil, "and let's find a way to get behind that shrubbery before five."

#   #   #

Around 4:30, W.D. pulled his Taurus up to the St Luke's Cemetery gate and parked. He took out the black garbage bag and walked over to the Connally gravesite. He placed the bag right in the middle of the grave, turned and walked over to his car, backed out onto Highway 2 and headed to Erskine.

Meanwhile, the two agents were ensconced in the shrubbery and were not discernible to view. They both had their weapons on hand awaiting the evening and an almost sure pick up by the kidnappers.

"Well, it's certainly not going to happen right at 5:00," said Andersen. "Hope we don't have to be scrunched in here until midnight."

"Huh, yeah, I wonder if they'll drive in or walk in." Nelson shifted to his left side as he moved off a lower limb of a lilac bush.

Around six, they were shocked to hear sirens and then to see a patrol car pull into the cemetery. It drove right up to the Connally gravesite and a policeman got out of the car headed for the black bag while the other remained in the car.

"Good God," said Emil, "they're East Grand Forks policemen. What the hell are they doing here?"

Andersen stepped out of the shrubbery and said, "Hold it right there, I'm Agent Andersen, BCA, and this is Agent Nelson – you're interfering with the apprehension and arrest of two kidnappers."

"Oh, Jesus, you scared me. I'm Chief Otto Nyberg, of the East Grand Forks police. Ah, we're here because we got a call from my brother whose airport security at the Grand Forks Airport who said that a black Town Car is parked in the passenger lot. Witnesses stated that the two men that drove that car were seen boarding a Gulfstream Three Jet at around 5:30 headed for Las Vegas."

"So, what the hell are you doing here?" Nelson didn't get the connection.

"We heard via an APB that the kidnappers in a black Lincoln Town Car had dropped off Lance Haskins at his home in Erskine," said Nyberg, "so I called Preston and he told me about the ransom…ah, so we thought we'd better see if they'd picked up the black bag – before some other interested parties decided to root around here." Larry Preston was head of the BCA and monitoring the kidnapping from the St. Paul Office.

Chief Nyberg looked apologetic. "Hey, I'm sorry; I've pushed myself into your jurisdiction here."

Andersen stared at Nyberg. "What do you mean? Kidnappers dropped off Lance Haskins? Is he alive and well?" He swore under his breath. "That little boy's got to be taken to the hospital. Pronto. Was he harmed or abused in any way?"

"Well, no word on his condition, but I think we'd have heard if he'd been mistreated." Nyberg looked concerned.

"The big question now is why didn't the alleged kidnappers pick up the black bag?" Nelson looked over at Andersen, "don't you think we should radio this into Preston?"

"Yup, right away."

"You'd better call Sheriff Bahnrude before you call Preston," Nyberg motioned him over to his squad car. "You know what a stickler old Lar is about detail and sequential action."

Andersen stepped over to the squad car and radioed the sheriff.

"Ah, say sheriff, Agent Andersen here. What's the latest on the kidnappers? Huh? No one has picked up the black bag. Ah, yes, Chief Otto Nyberg tried to. Ah huh. He'll tell you about it. What's the deal on Lance? Was he dropped off at home? Did you get him checked out? What? God Almighty? You are kidding me? What? Now, I've heard everything. Yeah. Wow! Gotta report all this to Preston. Over and out."

Chief Nyberg and Agent Nelson looked at Andersen in anticipation. "What the hell is up, man?" Nelson was impatient for news.

"Well Bahnrude told me that the kidnappers, two big guys in a black Town Car, dropped Lance off around 4:30 this afternoon at his home. His mother was at work. Neighbors reported that they also dropped off a yellow lab puppy, a red bicycle, and tons of dog food and dog toys. They heard Lance say good-bye to them and call them Uncle Max and Uncle Sheldon."

"That's the craziest thing I've ever heard of?" Nelson was flabbergasted. "Say, is somebody pulling a prank here – filming this for a TV show?"

Chief Nyberg and the patrolman were speechless. The black bag still lay in the middle of the gravesite, almost forgotten in the latest development.

Andersen continued, "W.D. brought Lance to the emergency room for a checkup and X-rays. No problem of any kind. Seems well nourished and no sign of bruising. But his mother, on the other hand, met them in the lobby and fainted on the spot. She had to be resuscitated and is now going to spend the night in the hospital under sedation. The Caldwell's are taking care of Lance."

Andersen sat down on his haunches and said, "Anybody got a flask?"

Everybody laughed, but no one moved. Soon Andersen got up and walked over to Nyberg's squad car, got in, and used the car phone to call in his report to Preston in St. Paul. After that, he grabbed the black bag, motioned to Emil, and they all set out for W.D.'s office. Both the agents were glad the kidnapping had come to a happy conclusion.

# # #

Late that afternoon the clouds beneath the luxurious Gulfstream Jet were rimmed with a rosy hue from the setting sun. Max and Sheldon were on board and had just helped themselves to some Bristol Sherry.

"You know, I'm glad this whole fiasco ended well, at least for little Lance," Sheldon looked at Max, "I'm going to miss the little guy."

"Yeah, he's a smart one," Max looked sad, "wish I'd had a little grandson of my own."

"Huh, how did we get the wrong info on him – he's not even related to W.D.?" Sheldon thought for a moment. "Probably came from Sniderman."

They were both distressed and Sheldon was overly anxious about the way events went in McIntosh. Would the Boss see no signed contract and no ransom money as failure to complete the job?

"Say, Max, what's this?' Sheldon pushed up against a large envelope marked 'Urgent' with a logo of two crows on it. He opened it quickly and pulled out a neatly typed contract. He handed it to Max.

"Oy! This is our next assignment for the boss. Over in Benedict Canyon next week."

"What! You understand all this gibberish?" Sheldon had never worked on this level of criminality before.

"Oh, yeah. Should be easy. I can put the plans together tonight when we get back to Calabasas. No problem."

Max eased back in his seat and took a light snooze.

13

"Good morning. My name is Dyanna Dahlberg and I'm a new employee," I spoke slowly, enjoying the sound of it. I was in a long line of individuals, waiting to be admitted to the glorious world of television production. I was surprised by how long it took to get my job at Capital Broadcasting System. It had been in the hands of my agent Arnold Thorne and took almost six weeks until I stepped into the lobby as a fully fledged employee.

"Yes, Ms. Dahlberg, I have your I.D. right here," said the security guard, a tall, thin man in a black uniform. He was neat and efficient and at ease behind a desk with a clear bulletproof panel. "You are to report to Mr. Wade Tarintina in Documentary Film Department." He turned and beckoned to a young man behind him. "This is Helmet Berget, Mr. Tarintina's assistant."

Helmet stepped forward and clasped my hand, "Welcome to CBS, Ms. Dahlberg, please follow me."

We stepped inside a large elevator headed for the fourth floor. I wondered what Wade Tarintina was really like? I'd only read one profile of him in a broadcast trade magazine when he was in his radio career.

I had taken special care of my appearance today. Unlike most young female executives, I was not wearing a tailored dress or a suit. I had on an expensive pair of white silk trousers and a thousand-dollar tennis sweater. I wore white flats and diamond earrings and just had my hair cut short at the Vidal Sassoon Hair Salon in Beverly Hills.

We got off the elevator and I followed Helmet along a hallway covered with large photographs of television greats, sitcom stars, and various executives.

Wade Tarintina was standing up behind his massive desk with a big smile on his face. He quickly came around to greet me as I stepped thru the doorway.

"My goodness, it's so great to meet you, Dyanna. I have such a good feeling about you and your contribution to our team," he spoke with a surprising Southern accent. He motioned for me to sit down in a small leather chair situated alongside his desk. I took a quick look around and saw that his office was far from neat; it had a lived-in look. Small piles of manuscripts, VHS video cassettes, and photos were stacked around the room.

Just then, a red-haired intern wheeled a coffee cart with a silver warming dish into the room. She filled our cups discreetly and then left. Tarintina did not glance at the coffee, but began telling me about CBS Television Studios, starting with a quick background, and then how recently they'd hit a slump, but were now up and running again. They'd developed a new direction, hired a new CEO, and were switching from producing sitcoms to documentary television specials. He cited his admiration for producer Ken Burns whose documentaries had appeared on PBS.

"I understand you're developing a three-parter on the

illegal growing of marijuana in the Emerald Triangle," I said to let him know I'd been reading the trades.

"Well, no, Dyanna…uh…actually that was shut down…for right now. We've had problems with renewing the option on the book the script was based on. The author Aldean Matheson wanted more money than we offered him. But, it looks like we'll be buying the rights to another book – ah, by him – called *The New Moccasin Game*. So, we'll be devoting time and advertising dollars to a documentary about Indian casinos."

"Oh, I didn't know that gaming was a national movement among tribes."

"Yeah it is. The Supreme Court Ruling on the Seminoles has changed everything."

I was surprised to hear that CBS Television was picking up on this trend already. Mother and I had recently visited the building site of the Silver Star Casino on NW Minnesota's Ojibwa Reservation and been impressed by the hope it offered the tribe.

"Dyanna, uh, I have to mention here that there's another person for you to meet his morning…our CEO, Samuel C. Walberg, who actually is the one who hired you."

"Oh, that's interesting." I was surprised. "I've never met him; at least, I don't think so."

"Oh, he's had you thoroughly investigated and he's impressed, so don't worry. You won't be on display and judged."

But this news really put me on edge. I nervously ran my fingers through my short hair, took another sip of the now cold coffee, as Helmet appeared suddenly at the door.

"Are you ready to meet Mr. Walberg?"

I stood up. "Oh, yes, I am." I followed Helmet to the elevator and we proceeded to the fifth floor.

We entered an exquisitely decorated anteroom, painted in shades of pale peach offset by a lovely dark mahogany brown and amber Persian rug.

"Dyanna Dahlberg, this is Marite, Mr. Walberg's secretary." Helmet deftly made introductions to the large, plus-sized woman of indeterminate age; her long blonde hair turned under and diamond earrings flashing their authenticity.

"So good to meet you, Dyanna, welcome to CBS. Mr. Walberg is waiting to meet you please follow me."

She knocked lightly, and then opened the door and we stepped into the cavernous office of the CEO. She turned and left, softly closing the door. I began what seemed like the longest walk of my life across the room. Unlike Mr. Tarintina, the rather small figure of Mr. Walberg, ensconced behind his desk, did not stand up to greet me.

He watched me silently and indicated a chair in front of his desk. He still did not say anything.

"Mr. Walberg, it's my pleasure to meet you. I'm looking forward to joining the documentary team here."

"Yes. Good morning, Dyanna...so nice to make your acquaintance," Mr. Walberg's voice was soft and stealthy. "Thank you for making your way up here and I have every indication that you will be a great addition to CBS Television Studios." I noticed his gray hair was cut in a military style and his desk was almost bare except for a sheet of white paper and a fountain pen.

As I was about to respond, the door opened and his secretary stepped in. "Ms. Dahlberg, Helmet is here to escort you to the business office and then back to Mr. Tarintina."

I stood up. Mr. Walberg did not.

It seemed like an even longer walk back to meet Helmet, who was waiting in the anteroom. We were soon on our way to the business office on third floor where I signed some tax forms. My contract had already been signed a few days ago, so we returned to Mr. Tarintina's office.

Now it was time to make some notes during my talk with Wade. I'd started thinking of him by his first name because of his informality and our closeness in age. While he was taking a call, I had a chance to study him. He was a handsome man, no doubt about it. His dark curly hair was cut in a perfect style for him, balanced out by longer sideburns. He was easily six feet and knew how to dress. He'd removed his tie earlier in our discussion and could carry this off without looking disheveled. His most attractive feature was his smile, so slow to start, then eyes trained on my face, it continued to radiate into a jubilance no words could express.

"Well, Dyanna, you've survived our orientation. I'd like to mention a few key things now. I plan to have you work down on the first floor for the first month or two. You will have a cubicle there alongside other staffers, researchers, and interns. You'll be introduced as a researcher; so get to know them on a day-to-day basis."

"Oh, yes, that's a good idea. I'm all for it. Do you have a job description for researcher?"

"Of course. I have it right here." As he continued to fill me in on particulars, I was very impressed by his overall concern for me and I looked forward to working at CBS Television.

"So that concludes my visits with you today, Dyanna. I've arranged for a full tour of the studios that will take approximately two hours. Then a car and driver will be waiting at Gate 8 to take you back to your hotel."

Then almost as an afterthought, he leaned in toward me, "Dyanna, I want you to know that Mr. Walberg really liked you...he loved what you were wearing." He looked closely at me. "Today you met one of the most powerful homosexuals in the business."

14

Wade Tarintina opened his large front door with his old-fashioned key, and purposely delayed entering his living room. He paused to look around. He was so pleased by the décor, the way the setting sun played off against the crystal chandelier; and enormously gratified that he could afford to own this house.

He quickly ran up the stairs to the second-floor master bedroom, whipped around to the closet, hung up his jacket and slipped out of his trousers, hanging them up next to the other pants. He reached into the casual closet for his Levis' and a denim shirt. He loved his Birkenstock sandals and planned to wear them someday soon with one of his suits.

As Tarintina slowly made his way back downstairs and into the living room, he thought about his day. It was such a pleasure to meet Dyanna Dahlberg. She was lovely and gracious and he knew she'd fit into his research team. Suddenly he had a sharp pang of anxiety. The pipeline documentary was not coming together. He'd been turned down for an interview and filming by Environ-Oil in Oxnard.

He'd been the major force behind buying the rights to the book that the documentary was based on. It was brilliant and its author Aldean Matheson had a bestseller, a real hit on his hands with *The Scandalous Odyssey of an Oil Tycoon*, a book that exposed the locations and impact of the Los Angeles oil fields with derricks pumping day and night, many of them right near homes, schools, and churches. The executives at Environ-Oil knew he had just purchased the television rights and that CBS was set to produce it, because it had been in all the trades.

He stretched out on his velvet chaise and allowed himself a few minutes of reflection. Being involved with the oil documentary brought back memories of his childhood. It was painful to think back over the years that he'd lived in the projects of Baldwin Hills. He knew he would never forget the rotten-egg smell that filled the air around the apartment he'd shared with his aunt – the smell that gave him a headache, a sore throat, and nausea. The smell that came from growing up in close proximity to the fumes from the derricks and pump jacks hidden behind a big stucco wall and working 24 hours a day. Unbeknownst to him, the gaseous odor was caused by fracking and acidization that allowed the oil to rise to the surface. Unbeknownst to him, it made him sick. Unbeknownst to him, it would shorten his life.

He got hold of himself just before a major panic attack occurred. He had what was called a migraine with an aura that caused disturbed vision and speech. The migraines were only one of a number of high-risk seizures he endured. His high-priced doctors told him it was caused by his early exposure to the dangerous fumes from the oil pumps. No one talked about the fumes when he was growing up, or if they did, no one did anything about them. Like the palm trees; not native to L.A., they were just accepted.

He'd lived with his granny Nina in her little cottage as a child, so he was told. But one morning he'd awakened to find that granny was gone. An older man with bifocals and overalls came into his bedroom and had him pack a little bag. He took him by the hand, and led him out to an old vehicle and drove day and night to deliver little Wade to the Los Angeles Orphan Asylum. At the age of nine, little Wade was sent to live with a relative in the Baldwin Hills project of Los Angeles. His aunt Maxine was willing to take him because she got a monthly check from the child welfare system for his care.

Maxine was a jazz dancer and gone most evenings – sometimes not coming home at all. She had told Wade that his parents had been killed in a car accident. She invented stories about how rich his father was and what a beautiful mother he had. But little Wade knew his parents were cartoon characters made up by Maxine to discipline him when he was naughty or to keep him from telling the child welfare agent that she was never there.

He escaped at age sixteen by just walking out carrying the little suitcase he'd had as a child. With his good looks and low mellow voice, he moved quickly into the entertainment world. He'd started by washing dishes in a bar and later helped book the groups that played there. He knew how to take care of himself and was good with handling money.

Now he was a big-time television producer. Now he had a chance to get revenge. Those oil fields, with derricks and pump jacks, just a few feet from the front door of the homes and schools needed to be exposed. The world should see this side of Los Angeles. And he was the right one to expose them.

#   #   #

Wade quickly shook out his pills from a well-used bottle, swallowing them dry, sighing as they took effect. He treasured his time alone; he needed to mull things over. No girlfriend had been invited to move in with him. He only made an exception for his devoted staff. Every Friday night he had an open house for them to drop by, use the pool, and enjoy snacks and the bar. Sometimes it was really late before they broke up.

Tonight he planned to spend some time in the garden. He'd had it planted with some of his favorite flowers – purple Iris, white peonies, and lilac bushes – amidst a mat of Montana thistle and local canyon ferns. His pool and cabana were meticulously maintained by the Sawyer Brothers. On the way out, he glanced at his telephone and recording device. It was glittering with messages, twelve calls so far. He'd handle them a bit later. This was his favorite time of day – dusk – when day was transitioning into night.

As Wade was about to open the back door he heard his front doorbell chimes. He smiled. They were based on the theme from the Delta 500 and always bode excitement. It must be a staff member, he thought.

Instead a tall man of middle age stood there staring at him.

"Are you Wade Tarintina?"

"Why, yes, I am." Wade noticed the man's cheap wig and wondered what that was about.

"Mr. Tarintina, someone wants to talk to you. It's urgent… please step over to the car."

Wade hesitated. He did not recognize the man in the car either. He appeared to be an older, heavyset man, wearing dark glasses and a poorly adhered moustache.

"Are you guys lost?"

"No sir, please step over to the car."

Wade was in a good mood until he noticed how close they'd parked to his new black Porsche Cabriolet on the left hand side of the courtyard. Now he was becoming annoyed.

"What do you guys want?"

Suddenly the man behind him swung a billy club and hit Wade hard in the back of the head. He fell to his knees and actually started to see stars. In a moment, a velvety blackness enveloped him and he fell flat on his face. The tall man turned and eased back into the passenger side, just before the driver of the gray Saab backed up, accelerated, and aimed straight at the prone figure. THUMMMMP, the car screeched as it hit Wade's body, and then made a sharp right turn, shot through the driveway, onto Benedict Canyon Drive, and sped away.

#   #   #

At ten o'clock the lights on Wade's property were timed to turn on. A small spotlight lit the large Arizona cactus, to the right of the entrance, and created a dramatic ambience. The big oak door stood open, ready for visitors to enter Wade's lovely home, the black Porsche shimmered, a symbol of the owner's successful status, and on the ground near it, laid the perfectly placed form of a man displayed as if in a scene from an Agatha Christie murder mystery, faced-down, his arms spread out, and his legs akimbo, one Birkenstock dyed red by his blood.

The security team arrived just as the lights turned on. They drove into the lighted courtyard and could not believe their eyes. "Jeez! My God isn't that Wade? Ah – is he lying in a pool of blood?"

The driver started to imperceptibly shiver. This was what he hated most about his job: the possibility of violent crime. His partner grabbed the car phone and called 911. She reached the West Los Angeles County Police Department dispatcher: "Say, we have an emergency here at a residence on Benedict Canyon Drive. The owner Wade Tarintina is lying in his courtyard bleeding profusely; it would seem he's been attacked – or worse – dead. No, I don't know. We have not seen anyone else. We are his security team, Anderson & Albrecht. Yes, we usually start at ten and do all-nighters. Yes, that's the right address. For God's sake! Hurry."

The team jumped out of the car to attend to Wade. They checked his pulse and tried to see if they could administer first aid and then took out their camera and took some photos.

# # #

Sirens rent the air as the Los Angeles Fire Department from Station #71 and an ambulance turned into the courtyard dispatching a gaggle of men who swarmed the property. A police car squeezed in and two patrolmen stepped out and immediately took charge. The first patrolman went directly to the door of the home, pistol drawn, and stepped in to check the premises. He found nothing amiss on the first floor; the upstairs bedroom and baths were secure. The back door was still locked and as he stepped into the garden; he checked the cabana and low stone fence, and found no one.

Actually there was no evidence of anyone being on the property except the victim. He pulled out a big roll of yellow crime tape and encircled the property and then joined the second patrolman, who was assisting the EMT's with identifying the unconscious man. They'd found a wallet in the back pocket of his Levi's that gave his name and address. Also a medical card for organ donation and blood type as well as whom to call in an emergency. After the EMT's had loaded the victim onto a gurney, the officer knew it was time to call the station to request back up and a crime scene investigator.

The patrolmen watched as the taillights of the ambulance turned left on Benedict Canyon Drive headed for the Cedars-Sinai Emergency Room with the almost lifeless body. The fire truck followed.

Soon two investigators swerved in and parked. "So what went on here?" Phillip Jessup stepped forward with Dwight Stilton right behind him. "Sure is a lot of blood – was the vic stabbed?"

"No, he seems to have been coshed on the back of the head – I've got the billy club used in an evidence bag," said the patrolman. "It appears he was run over by a vehicle after being bashed."

"Good God," said Stilton, "did they mean to kill him with the car?"

"Yeah, I'd say so," said the patrolman, "but they missed the body and just ran over his arm, hitting an artery, which explains the huge amount of blood. There are tire impressions on his skin and black rubber on his shirt sleeve."

"Who is he?"

"Ah, a big time TV Producer and former radio personality by the name of Wade Tarintina," said the first patrolman.

"I've got his wallet and ID here," said the second patrolman as he passed it over to Jessup,

"It has someone listed to call in an emergency…could be a brother or a son?"

"Hmm. Yeah, a Helmet Berget, better check him out,

Dwight, and give him a call. Meet him over at the emergency room and interview him."

"Okay. Maybe I'll bring him in for questioning."

15

"Um, good evening, I'm Helmet Berget, the medical emergency contact for Mr. Wade Tarintina. How's he doin'? Ah, here's my ID." Helmet was very worried and his anxiety was not well hidden. His palm literally shook as he handed over the card to the male receptionist at Cedars-Sinai Emergency Room.

"Thank you for getting here tonight." The receptionist looked at the card, "Dr. Throgstad wants to talk with you." He turned and pointed to a glassed-in office. "The triage nurse will process you in there and then the doctor will be with you." He turned away to greet another visitor.

"Have a seat please. Are you Helmet Berget?" The nurse motioned him to come in.

"Yes, ma'am, I am."

"Are you related to Mr. Tarintina?"

"No, I am his assistant at CBS Studios."

"Well, we are waiting for his family to arrive so I am not sure what part you will play."

"Mr. Tarintina does not have any close family members. That's why he appointed me."

"Well, hmm, we just received a call from a woman who said she was his wife – a Regina Tarintina – and that she'd be here within the hour to meet with the doctor."

That really threw Helmet. He stood up to get his bearings. "I think not. No. Mr. Tarintina is divorced – rather acrimoniously – he would not want his ex-wife here or even allow her to know the extent of his injuries!"

The nurse looked at him and said, "Oh really? Please have seat in the waiting room while I look into this."

Helmet decided to call Wade's attorney on the lobby pay phone and left a message. He asked him to call and notify the police of the restraining order on Wade's ex-wife. Again anxiety set in as he sank down into a large vinyl sofa. He heard a person clear their throat and looked up to see a man in a dark overcoat staring down at him. "You are Helmet Berget?"

"Yes sir, I am."

"I'm Detective Dwight Stilton of the LAPD. Humph, awfully young aren't you, for this kind of responsibility? Are you related to Mr. Tarintina?"

"No, sir, I work for him at CBS Television Studios. I'm not that young – I've graduated with a Masters in theatre from Yale University and have worked for several years at a top talent agency here in L.A. before joining CBS."

"Well, thanks for arriving so quickly... it's obvious Mr. Tarintina trusts you."

"Yes, he does. I would like to talk to Wade's doctor. I am very concerned about what's happened to him."

"Certainly. But I will need to talk with you. Oh, here comes a doctor now."

The doctor walked over to Det. Stilton. "You are Mr. Berget?"

"Oh, no. This is Mr. Berget." He stepped behind the

young man. "I'm a detective with the LAPD investigating the assault."

"Ah, sorry, greetings, Mr. Berget, I am Dr. Nils Throgstad and I have a quick update for you. Mr. Tarintina received several scans on his head as well as on his arm. We made a decision to perform surgery on the humerus and insert a metal plate. The humerus, in laymen's terms, is the large bone above the elbow and is the location of the severed brachial artery which contributed to his blood loss. This was also repaired." The doctor glanced away. "He should be back in the ICU soon to receive a blood transfusion."

Helmet was impressed by the non-emotional and calm report. It helped to allay his concerns. He nodded. "Then what is the category or definition of his injuries?"

"Well, I'd say serious, but not critical." The doctor turned quickly, and swept through a side door.

Just then, Helmet and the detective heard screaming and moaning coming from the elevator. A woman seemed to blow out of it into the waiting room, her long curly hair flying in all directions, her makeup smeared. Her long cape was covered with tassels; she fell on the floor and rolled herself up in it. She was wailing an indecipherable mantra. "Ohnya om…my man is dead, my man is dead. Oh, God help me. I can't live without him!"

Regina Tarintina had arrived.

16

I had a sense of foreboding as I stepped into the lobby of the CBS Studios. The genial guard was sober-faced and abrupt as he checked my ID and nodded to me to enter the workplace. As I stood in the doorway of the first-floor research unit I could see the anxiety and concern on the faces of my co-workers and knew it was related to the horrific attack on our boss.

I entered my cubicle, set my briefcase down on the desk and shoved my purse into the left hand drawer. Soon I was joined by three of the staff; they slipped stealthily into my cubicle, one at a time. Gervaise pulled up the stool, Sarah and Mavis took the folding chairs.

"Dy, did you hear about the assault on Wade Friday night?"

"Oh, yes I did," I said, "Helmet called me on Saturday night with the details."

"My God, Helmet? Why Helmet?" Mavis was puzzled. "What did he have to say?" All three of them were riveted by my reply.

"Yeah, well, it seems that Helmet was the Emergency Medical Contact for Wade and was on the scene within the hour. But he ran into trouble because Wade's ex-wife showed up and created a scene."

"What! His ex-wife? I didn't know Wade had been married," said Sarah.

"Oh yeah, she's a wacko," said Gervaise, "she's been suing him for money since their divorce two years ago."

"Oh, that's right," said Mavis, "She used to hang around the back entrance of CBS until Walberg banned her from the premises."

"Huh, yeah, Helmet said he had to call the police to enforce the restraining order filed by Wade about a year ago." I wondered how much I should divulge.

"I read that she got half of everything Wade owned – more than a million dollars – but she'd already run through it." Gervaise looked thoughtful. "Say, how is Wade doing, anyway?"

"He's serious, but not critical." I said.

They were all quiet, processing the information. Then Gervaise picked up the slack. "Did Helmet tell you who did it, er, what exactly happened?"

"Yes, he did somewhat. It seems Wade was set upon by a couple of unidentified men, one hit him on the back of the head as he stepped outside, and the second guy drove over him with the car."

"God! What? Drove over him? Who does stuff like that?" All three of them just stared at me in shock.

"You know, it's grisly, but it could have been worse. It seems that the assailant was a damn poor driver because he missed the body and only drove over Wade's arm, and broke it above the elbow."

"Jeez, how terrible. Do the doctors know when Wade can come back to work?" Mavis seemed on the point of tears.

"Maybe in a couple of weeks. Although I'm sure it will

be at least six months before the bone heals. I think Wade can describe the two guys when he's fully conscious," I said, "they seem to be members of the Gang that Couldn't Shoot Straight."

"Say, you don't think that ex-wife hired some nut jobs to take him out, do you?" Gervaise looked intently at me.

"Well, yeah, she could have. She'd better have an alibi," I said.

"You know, I was just thinking of another suspect – Aldean Matheson. Boy, he was in a rage over his cancelled book option," said Gervaise. "He didn't get the money he wanted and said he was going to kill Wade."

"Was that the book about the pipelines?" Mavis looked around for an answer.

"Oh no, it was about the illegal growing of marijuana in the Emerald Triangle," said Gervaise, "So now we're back with the Indian Casinos."

"Guess I should mention we just got a notice that a BCA agent is arriving here next week – he's an expert on marijuana," announced Sarah. "His name is W.D. Caldwell."

"Oh, I know him. He's not a BCA agent – he was an informant for the agency," I said, "and he made a name for himself by helping bust up a huge drug network." I was surprised to hear he was still coming out to L.A. since the documentary was shelved. But, it would be good to have his calming presence in these tense times.

"What about Aldean – has he been brought in for questioning?" Mavis looked hopeful.

"Well, he made threats against Tarintina," said Gervaise. "But, he'd caught a flight back to Long Island early that Friday evening – so maybe he has an alibi."

# # #

A few weeks later, prior to Wade's returning to work, Walberg was busy planning his next move. He was angry that there'd been no arrest by the LAPD in the assault on Tarintina. He picked up his interoffice line.

"Marite, please place this call for me," he cited a telephone number off a card. "Buzz me when you have him on the line. Thank you."

A half hour later Marite buzzed her boss. "Mr. Walberg, Christian Handler on the line."

"Mr. Handler, I want to hire you to investigate the assault on one of our employees, the director Wade Tarintina. Yes, that's right. Yes. No problem. I want to get started immediately. Yes, I'll sign. Tomorrow morning. Thank you." He hung up without saying good bye.

He'd just hired the famous private detective agency, the Herschel Handler Agency of Malibu, known for their precise homicide investigations. Expensive? Yes. But he wanted a job done and done right.

17

"Oh, Mother, what a delight to hear from you. Tomorrow night? Yes, I understand and I'll be there to meet you."

My Mother, Gunhilde, was confirming her upcoming trip to Los Angeles for herself and Aunt Anita for a six-week stay with me.

"No, I couldn't be more pleased. I have lots of room."

It had taken me a month to settle into my new apartment, a condo located on Mulholland Drive. I couldn't believe all the amenities that it had.

We went on to discuss details of the trip, but Mother was surprised when I announced that I'd hired a car and driver to be at their beck and call.

When she continued to object, especially about the cost, I changed the subject. "Guess what, Mother, I got a call from a BCA Agent in St Paul named Jon Andersen who plans to visit me, too."

She replied with a giggle.

"How did you know? Oh, I see – he called you for my number?"

"Well, tell Aunt Anita to pack some warm clothes as it gets cold out here in L.A. especially in the evening. Okay. Love you, too."

After I hung up, I started thinking about the recent assault on my boss. The wonderful, kind, and magical Wade Tarintina. As I looked around the apartment, I mentally thanked him for finding this condo for me, arranging the terms of the lease with his lawyer, and helping me move in. I wondered if his assault was work related. If so, was I at risk? Other co-workers? What was going on? I knew I would feel more secure after Mother and Aunt Anita arrived.

#

Two days after arriving in Los Angeles, Gunhilde and Anita felt like exploring the neighborhood. They called the car service and set up an appointment for that day.

Around one in the afternoon, they were picked up by Dyanna's car service. The driver, an older man, was attired in a uniform that looked like safari gear.

"Good afternoon, my name is Cecil and Miss Dahlberg asked me to drive you through the neighborhood, to get to know the streets, and see some of the residences."

He looked down at his large feet shod in light leather hiking boots.

"Why, thank you, Cecil, I'm sure it will be wonderful to get a chance to tour this neighborhood," said Aunt Anita, wondering what was missing in this man's life that he dressed like a big game hunter. Did he need to live out a fantasy through his clothes?

The sister's were set to depart; each had their purse and an energy drink, ready to go. Cecil was a bit taken aback. He was used to a lot of hesitation in his assigned pick-ups, fussing with their hair or not sure what to wear.

"Well, very good, I'm sure," he said.

He assisted them getting into the back seat of the car, adjusted the air conditioning, and handed them each a map with red circles around a few residences.

"My goodness," said Gunhilde, "there are some large properties here."

"Yes, ma'am, some of the top movie stars have homes in this area. Marlon Brando and Jack Nicholson, actually live a couple of blocks away."

He drove the Mercedes with one hand while sticking his left arm out the window pointing at houses.

"This is the driveway to Jack Nicholson's estate." He started to recount information on Nicholson and his girlfriend. He continued driving and commenting on homes of various lesser known stars.

"I hope we can visit Gary Cooper's home," said Gunhilde as she looked out the back window. She was surprised by how hilly and winding the road was. "My, you'd have to be a good driver to find your way home here, especially at night."

"Yeah, you're right," said Cecil, "many people aren't and have gone over the side."

He made a turn on Cielo Drive, slowing the car down. He turned onto a paved road up to a gated property and parked.

"Ladies, you can look through the gate bars into the front entrance of the mansion where Sharon Tate and her husband Roman Polanski lived."

He then went on to recount its history. "Actually it's where Sharon Tate and her friends were murdered by the Manson Gang." He looked back to see their response.

"What do you mean?" Aunt Anita was curious, "are you talking about a movie?"

He didn't answer.

"You know, we're from Minnesota, uh, we don't see many

movies," added Gunhilde.

"Well, no ma'am, this was real life – a shiftless bunch of homeless types killed the residents of this house." He was surprised that there were people who'd actually never heard of this crime. "They were allegedly sent out with knives and guns by a man named Charles Manson to break in and murder everyone in the house." He concluded by saying, "they stabbed and killed the movie actress Sharon Tate who was eight months pregnant, and her three friends." He turned to look at the women, concerned that they might have questions for him that he couldn't answer.

He was surprised to see that they were speechless. Gunhilde was staring at the brown shingled house, unable to express her feelings. Aunt Anita started rocking back and forth, moaning softly.

"Oh driver, this is too much for us. Please take us back to the condo." Gunhilde started shaking.

"Ladies, what is wrong, did I say something that offended you?" Cecil was getting upset. Actually he hadn't told them about the other victim, an eighteen-year old visitor to the property.

"Oh no," said Aunt Anita, "it's just that this house looks exactly like the house my niece owned in Minnesota and – well, hers was not as big – and she, too, had been troubled by drifters, odd kinds of people, breaking in."

"Oh my God, yes, it's quite a shock to think of what might have happened back then," said Gunhilde. Her heart beating fast, as it dawned on her that Dyanna might have been murdered, too. She thought of the notorious neighbor Steve Olsen, reputed drug dealer, who'd been seen on her property several times. They headed back to Dyanna's condo.

No more sightseeing for them.

18

"Please come this way, Mr. Handler," the CBS guard pointed to a young man,
"Mr. Berget will escort you to the various departments as per Mr. Walberg's request. Have a nice day."

"Thank you," said Handler. "Are you Mr. Berget?"

"Oh, yes, I am. Sorry, I guess I was expecting a much older man."

"Oh, perhaps, you were expecting my late uncle Herschel Handler? I'm his nephew."

"Oh, yes, I was." He immediately applied himself to the business at hand. "The first place we'll stop, sir, is the business office. Franklin Grant, the head of that department, has some paperwork for your signature and then a stop in Tarintina's research department."

They strode to the elevator and were soon on their way up. They were met on the third floor by a short, heavyset man in his early forties. His hair was a color Handler had never seen before. It was between red and black and must have been highlighted by a stylist with a sense of humor.

"Good morning, Mr. Handler, please step into my office. Helmet will wait here in the lobby for you."

Handler usually sent his clients a contract and then they

negotiated it – sometimes taking a week or more to nail down the terms and payment. Walberg must have researched PI contracts because he had anticipated all the areas where Handler usually had to compromise. He could not believe how well written it was; very much in his favor. He read it twice, three times. He signed it with a flourish with his Uncle Herschel's famous pen. Then Grant handed him a company check for the full amount of the investigation. It was written for twice Handler's already high fee. Attached to the check was a small note with Walberg's name and title. It read "*I want you to nail the son-of-a bitch.*"

"Well, I'm looking forward to meeting Mr. Walberg," said Handler, "he really gets right down to business."

"Oh, he's not going to meet you. He has complete confidence in you and will stay in touch by telephone. He was a dear friend of your uncle's," said Grant. "So nice to have met you," he turned away leaving Handler no time to ask any more questions.

Somewhat surprised by the cancelled meeting, Handler met Berget by the elevator. He wished he could have an espresso before the next appointment. He'd never done business like this before.

# # #

Soon they were on their way to the research department on the first floor where Wade's staff worked.

"The research department has ten employees, all handpicked by Mr. Tarintina, to do research, interviews, and write script drafts of the various documentaries in production by CBS," said Berget. "It's quite a busy operation, probably similar to that of a newspaper."

As they stepped into the large department with various cubicles, Handler thought the noise level was extremely high, but it felt invigorating. He turned just in time to see a tall, blonde woman heading his way with gorgeous full lips.

"Mr. Handler, we've been expecting you. My name is Dyanna Dahlberg and I'm a researcher here along with nine others. Mr. Walberg said you wanted to briefly interview us about the assault on our boss."

"Very nice to meet you, *Signorina*," he said flirtatiously, "please call me Christian. Yes, I do want to interview you and the others as to who might be a possible suspect and get some timelines."

Just then an older man stepped out from behind Dyanna and stood looking at Handler. She quickly made introductions.

"Oh, I'm sorry. Mr. Handler – er – Christian, this is Mr. W.D. Caldwell, from Erskine, Minnesota. He was hired by Wade as an expert for a documentary on the Emerald Triangle, that's now in a holding pattern."

"Pleased to meet you, Mr. Handler, I've worked for the Minnesota BCA as a mercenary informant on an illegal drug cartel investigation and a murder. We had one of the biggest drug busts in Minnesota...."

"Pleased to meet you, too, W.D.," Handler promptly dismissed him by looking over to the left side of the room.

W.D., unconcerned by the rejection, started a monologue on his abilities. Suddenly Handler turned to stare at him, but said nothing. W.D. continued. Finally it became embarrassing and Handler's silence became apparent even to W.D. He stopped abruptly.

"Well, I've got to get on my way. My wife is waitin' on me. Nice to meet you, Mr. Handler." He turned to say goodbye to Dyanna, but Handler reached out and put his hand on his shoulder.

"Oh, wait just a moment, sir, are you busy tomorrow?" He looked at W.D. with a sparkle in his eye. "I have a job for you that'll start ASAP."

W.D. who was a big believer in *carpe diem* faced Handler and said, "No, I'm not busy. Where would you like to meet?"

"Ms. Dahlberg, we'll have to re-schedule the interviews today. We've run out of time. I will get back to you as to a date." Handler shook hands with W.D., handed him a card, and then bowed to Dyanna and said, "*Sei bellissima.*" With perfect timing Berget held the door open for the elevator and Handler stepped in. The door closed and they were gone.

19

Chris Handler was sopping wet; he'd been out on the beach enjoying an early swim and half-hour run. He stepped up onto the travertine courtyard of his home in Malibu and headed for the outdoor shower. He turned on the hot water, stripped down, washed off, and quickly grabbed a towel. He decided to dress casually and took a pair of white walking shorts and a white tee from the clothing bin. He glanced in the mirror, combed his wet hair straight back and decided not to shave – it was a 1930's look he liked.

As he took the broad stairs to his second-floor home office, his eyes never left the soft blue haze of the Santa Monica Mountain Range. He settled into his chair and was immediately taken over with plans for the day. He picked up the extension phone and buzzed his secretary.

"Tabitha, good morning, please arrange for David to pick up W.D. Caldwell at the Beverly Hills Hotel, Suite 16 – yes, he's alone – and bring him back here. Oh yes, that's right. Oh, and I'll need the conversation with Mr. Caldwell tape recorded – so please arrange that. Hmm, yes, he will be staying for lunch. Whatever… you order it. Serve us out by the pool. Anything for me to sign? Other than checks?

Okay."

While he waited for the arrival of W.D., he decided to re-read the newspaper accounts of Wade's assault. Then he reviewed the LAPD reports. He picked up the outside line and dialed a well-known number.

"Hey Dwight, Chris here – uh huh, no kidding. Just reviewing the reports on Wade Tarintina's assault. That's right. I have a question. Does Regina Tarintina have an alibi for Friday night? I mean before she showed up in the emergency room? What! She was a patient at Cedars-Sinai? A 5150? Yeah, I know. An involuntary commitment of individuals who present danger to themselves and others. Well, I guess that's as good an alibi as one can get. Huh? I guess that explains how she got to the ER so fast. Later. *Ciao amico.*"

W.D. was very impressed by the drive up Decker Road and as he looked out the rear window of the Jeep Wrangler YJ he felt like he was in a state park. It was so beautiful and untouched.

"Uh, does Mr. Handler live up here alone?"

"Yes, sir, he does," said David, "quite a view to the left."

W.D. looked down at the beach below and then up at mountain range just ahead. It was breathtaking.

"My goodness, he must do awfully well in his business to afford this," he mused.

"Oh, he does well, but Mr. Handler inherited the business and his home from his uncle – the late Herschel Handler – PI to the Stars. You may have heard of him?"

W.D. was stunned. "Yes, in fact, I have. Wasn't murder his specialty?"

"Yes, it was. His detection skills and insight were uncanny. I worked for him for many years."

They pulled into the driveway of a three-car garage. W.D. looked over at the neo-modern mansion tucked into the hillside sublimely immersed into the landscape of city, canyon, and ocean views. It was spectacular.

Chris met him at the large open entrance to the living room.

"Welcome W.D. – so good to see you again. I have coffee, mango juice, and scones, up in my office. Did you enjoy the ride out here?"

"I sure did. Thanks for picking me up." W.D. was actually starving and greatly appreciated the repast.

As they sipped coffee and munched on the scones, Chris gave W.D. a little insight into the Handler Agency.

"I run the company just like my uncle did; there's been no change since I took over about a year ago," he looked at W.D. with a twinkle in his eye. "But first, I want you to tell me about yourself – explain the work you did with the Minnesota BCA. Also if there's anything you're involved with now – criminal or otherwise – you'd like to share with me."

It wasn't often that W.D. had a chance to expound without restraint and he clearly relished the invitation. He told Chris about the marijuana gardens planted in a farming community by a religious family, his surveillance of Steve Olsen, a drug dealer, and the home invasion and murder of Olsen. He went on to tell Chris about buying Olsen's estate and the interest shown in it by pipeline companies. Lastly he told him about the strange and villainous efforts by R. Proctor Swinburne to buy the land; his disguises, and threats against W.D. to make him sell and his kidnapping of a small boy thought to be his grandson held for ransom.

After an hour non-stop, W.D. ran out of steam. He looked

over at Chris who had a mildly amused look on his face, but hadn't commented. "Thanks, son, I needed to get all that off my chest."

When W.D. leaned back in his chair, Chris realized he was a much older man than he first thought. He decided they both needed a break, and said, "Say, lunch is ready – what do you say we dine by the pool?"

"Why, yes, great – oh, this is the life. How wonderful to be able to work and live in such a stunning place."

They stood up, stretched, and headed downstairs to the patio. A table was set for dining and W.D. moved his chair so he could look out over the ocean below. Chris picked up the extension line on the nearby coffee table and requested lunch by the pool.

Soon, a young man appeared with a tray of chilled lemonade, followed by an avocado salad, and small bite-sized quiche. After settling in, Chris started telling W.D about himself and the Handler Company.

"The Handler Agency was started by my grandfather Delfonte Handler who had worked for Allan Pinkerton of the Pinkerton National Detective Agency around the turn of the century. He was not successful at first and just made enough to get by. He had two sons, my father Juergen and my uncle Hershel and neither was initially interested in working for Grandpa." He hesitated. "But my parents were killed just after WWII and due to a changing world; Hershel closed his musical revue and took over Grandpa's PI business.

"He adopted me after my parent's death in 1947 when I was just two years old. He never shared much about the company and I kind of came and went on my own. I attended Stanford University and have a Master's Degree in Italian

Studies and speak fluent Italian. I spent two summers in Milan working as an intern with a design firm."

"That's all very impressive," said W.D., "I noticed the language just rolls off your tongue." He thought of Chris's flirtatious greeting of Dyanna.

Chris smiled and said, "Why, thank you, W.D."

"But moving on," Chris refilled his glass of lemonade, "an overview of the Handler Agency: it's really hugely dependent on tipsters and a posse. First, tipsters. Their backgrounds are cleared and then they go to work at our Sunset office called Wheelock International Pipe Fitters. After hiring, they are given a packet that includes basic info on the cases we're working on and a telephone number that's answered 24 hours a day. They create their own networks and remain anonymous. They are only active in California and are paid by the number of tips they call in – whether they're used or not. Checks are sent out weekly."

He got up to stretch. Then moved over to the patio sofa and resumed his explanation. "The second part of our company is based on the posse concept. They are individuals who are paid to get information and evidence. They're usually street people who are under the radar – an old man with a cane, a college student with a backpack, or a young woman with a baby carriage sans baby."

"Why that's brilliant," said W.D.

"Uh, well it's not original. My uncle was impressed by the street urchins hired by Sherlock Holmes – the Baker Street Irregulars – paid to gather valuable information. My uncle called his version Handler's Posse. They show up in neighborhoods where the crime we're investigating was committed or hang out in the streets and cafes where the suspect or suspects live. They are not noticeable and many times have overheard conversations or noticed suspicious behavior that has lead to conviction."

He looked at W.D. to see how he was absorbing this information. "That, in fact, is what I have in mind for you."

W.D. looked interested, then puzzled. "Could you explain that a little more?"

"Yes, of course. There are only a few suspects in Wade Tarintina's assault. One I want checked out is Aldean Matheson. He was in negotiations with Wade for a new TV rights contract the day before the attack. CBS wouldn't meet his higher price and he was overheard making a threat on Wade's life."

"Hmm, yes, I can imagine a man might get upset over that. But not to the point of really killing someone."

"Well, he displayed suspicious behavior. According to my sources he left Los Angeles that Friday night. He had a woman with him. She was identified by the airlines as Joyce Santa Anna of Oxnard, California. A quick check revealed that she works for an oil refinery company."

"What I'd like you to do is surveil Matheson who lives in Montauk, Long Island. His comings and goings, visitors, and photos of him and this Joyce woman. Try to get inside his home and put a bug on his telephone. Ah, does this interest you?"

"Why it sure does. I'm in. Give me the details, son."

"You will be under contract for six months with an option to renew. You will have all expenses paid, a secure phone, and an ID card giving you the privileges of a private investigator with this company." He mentioned a fixed fee.

W.D. was surprised by the extent of the offer. He had fully expected to give advice, but not to be hired for a job like this.

"Chris, I would be honored to work for you. I would enjoy the job a whole lot. But are you sure you don't need a younger man for this?"

"No, you, your age, everything about you, W.D. is perfect. Let's go upstairs, sign the contract, and get your kit and expense money."

After signing, they shook hands. "W.D. in your leather kit is a roundtrip ticket to Long Island via La Guardia International Airport in New York, there is a secure line for you to call or Fax me, a special low-light camera for photos, and a life insurance policy that goes with the job."

"I am willing and ready to roll," said W.D., "I can't wait to get started."

"One last thing, you are free to do the job your way, hire any help necessary to aid and assist you, but remain incognito and under the radar."

"Perfectly clear."

"Let us have some dessert and a cup of espresso before you leave. Or if you're inclined, a glass of prosecco?"

"Ah, that sounds interesting – I suppose that's Italian liquor?" He watched as Chris poured some into small glasses.

"That's close; it's Italian white sparkling wine." They toasted one another. "So good to have you aboard, W.D."

Later, as Chris watched the older man get into the Jeep he thought just how fortuitous this accidental meeting was. Suddenly he was puzzled: who was this R. Proctor Swinburne? Maybe it was time to put Handler's Posse onto him?

20

It was early afternoon at Stony Brook University in Southampton, New York, the class was filled to the max, and chairs were set up in a circle so the students could see one another and Aldean Matheson could slip in and out of their vision. He looked forward to these one-off lectures. It felt like he was thinking out loud or like good conversation inviting his students to join him.

He was a sight to behold. He'd just returned from California and his appearance confirmed it. Long, hippie-length hair, graying at the temples, dressed in white linen slacks and a cotton white shirt, open at the throat to show off his hairy chest, sockless loafers; dressed in a casual counterpoint to his working man's face, with a large nose, uneven teeth with one gold filling, and laser-beam eyes. He lived a few dozen miles away along the beach in Montauk and this was a style of dressing he embraced.

Aldean lost a lot of points when students heard his voice: gravelly. But most annoying was his stutter. But it didn't seem to matter because he had so much great stuff to say about writing, how to go about it, why it mattered, and shared their dreams.

The class title was "The Environment in Fiction"and it relied heavily on research techniques and how to go about mastering them. Upton Sinclair's books were required reading.

"Good afternoon fellow writers. How many of you have read any of Upton Sinclair's books? Hmmm which ones?"

No one replied. They just stared at him. He moved right along pursuing the book titles without a response.

"Sinclair's books were all researched. For example, *The Jungle* was a book about an immigrant family and their dreadful working conditions in a meat packing company. He spent seven weeks working in one as background. He then spent months working in the coal fields of Colorado as research before writing two great books, *King Coal and The Coal War*. When he moved to California in 1927 he was inspired by Edward Doheny and ended up writing the best book ever titled *Oil!* on the topic of man's enrichment from petroleum fields deposited tens of millions of years ago."

The students all looked like they wanted to be someplace else.

"A-a-a-alright, let's get down to it. Your assignment is to write a short story based on the oil fields in Los Angeles," he looked at the class. Some were glassy-eyed, some were amused; others looked up disgustedly at the ceiling like, "My God, what next?"

"Ohhhh L.A. doesn't have oil fields, Dr. Matheson. Are you thinking of Dallas?"

"No, Martina, I'm not," Aldean was focused now, "we're going to go over some research themes for your short story. The plot, characters, POV, must all begin and end with the oil fields." He sucked on a Hall's cough drop seemingly lost in thought; then sitting down on a stool.

Students waited for an introduction. None came. "Okay. Let's take a break. Ten minutes." Aldean stood up and walked out the door.

He returned after fifteen minutes the class settled down and Aldean spoke without a stutter: "Tar seems have been known in the area from prehistoric times, and the Native American population of the Los Angeles basin used the tar for waterproofing and other purposes. The Spanish settlers used it for their lamps, as a sealant for roofs, and as grease for wagon wheels."

He walked around the room as if the news had just reached him. "However, it was Edward Doheny and his partner, Charles Canfield's oil well, begun on November 4, 1892, that brought the Los Angeles oil field into existence. They dug a well to 155 feet, halting because of the accumulation of toxic hydrogen sulfide gas in the hole." He hesitated and then moved behind the desk. "Doheny brought in a sharpened eucalyptus log and used it as an improvised percussion hammer to deepen the well, he punctured an oil reservoir, and began producing about seven barrels of crude a day."

"Dr. Matheson, how big was a barrel? What was it made of?"

"Good question, Sharon. A barrel is 42 gallons and the barrels back then were made of oak. Today, they're made of ribbed steel. Ah, they're still the standard oil measurement to this very day." He started coughing and then stepped out of the room.

He returned and picked right up. "Within a year of Doheny's well there were 121 wells on the field interspersed with homes and businesses, and the field's production reached 100,000 barrels. By the end of 1897, over 270 wells had been drilled into this new area." Aldean rapped his fingers on the desk. "Over the next two decades, Doheny would become wealthy beyond his wildest dreams."

Jeremy's hand shot up. "Dr. Matheson, I'm wondering… if all that oil is flowing…ah who's using it? How did Doheny make all that money?"

"Oil was sold to refineries to produce gas: this was extracted from crude to fuel the combustible engine and later the gasoline engine. Doheny was in the right place at the right time – from 1908 to 1927 – Henry Ford sold millions of Model T's, that ran on gasoline extracted from crude oil."

There was rustling in the room and whispering. Some kind of foment or reaction that Aldean knew could be tumultuous was brewing.

"We are coming to the end of the hour and I have three environmental fiction themes. Take your pick. But use one of them. First: write a short story about a young girl who is living in close proximity to thousands of oil and gas wells releasing toxic air contaminants near her home." Aldean waited for questions. There were none.

"Two: write a short story about a young couple who just bought a home near the Kenneth Hahn State Park, a welcoming oasis of green. They find out it sits adjacent to the Inglewood Oil Field, the second most productive field in the LA Basin." Again, Aldean waited for questions. None.

"Three: write a short story about how an older man whose dream was to live in L.A. discovered the truth about the trees and foliage that obscure the oil derricks. Look into the blue gum eucalyptus, and the palm tree, imported into Los Angeles in the 1800's to give the City a feel of a tropical Eden."

Aldean was ready to pack it in. "Oh, ah, papers due in a week with research citations. Good day."

The students gathered up their binders and notebooks and filed out of the room. Most were looking stunned. Three or four from New York City had that I Told You So look on their face while two students originally from Los Angeles were in a rage. So angry, they were just on the verge of attacking Dr. Matheson.

"I could kill that old bastard…those lies are incredible." Garvin glared at Matheson. But, he was close to graduating and did not want to be kicked out of class. His friend Ryan from Burbank, cast a scornful look at Aldean, but decided to wait until he got back to the dorm to open up on what he thought of the professor.

Aldean gathered up his briefcase and his lecture notes, closed the windows, and locked the doors. He headed out the back way where Stella was waiting in the Porsche. It was just another pissed-off class and he knew he was close to inciting a riot. But he could wait until the truth was known. Then the fun would begin.

21

W.D. excitedly took a flight out the next morning headed for Long Island. He had heard a lot about a place called Sag Harbor from Dyanna, and he was ready for it. For starters he was wearing walking shorts in tan twill and a matching short-sleeved shirt. When he arrived at LaGuardia, he was flagged by a dark-haired woman carrying a sign that merely stated 'W.D.' that she was waving up and down disinterestedly.

"I'm your man," he called out and flashed his driver's license. He was then escorted to a waiting black limousine ordered by Dyanna. He felt gleeful about the prospects of an adventure as he sank back into the luxurious leather seats and carefully pulled out a *Romeo Y Julieta* cigar from his valise.

A handsome, middle-aged man of Hispanic origins was at the wheel, "Greetings, I will be your driver, please sit back and enjoy your trip to Long Island, Mr. Caldwell." He thought the *un anciano* looked vaguely familiar, but then many of his passengers were celebrities or at least associated with fame.

As they rolled along, W.D. asked some pertinent questions about the local towns, especially one called Hicksville. The name amused him enormously.

"You know, I always wondered where all the hicks came from," said W.D. "Now I know." He grinned for no reason.

Dyanna had told him about the ocean beaches and he was thrilled to have a look at the long stretch of white sand just on the other side of Southampton. It made him think of Lake Superior, but it didn't come close to this magnificent body of water.

When they arrived in Sag Harbor he caught a glimpse of the impressive American Hotel. The driver pulled up to the front of entrance and opened the door. Then W.D. made a quick decision: It was too high profile for the work he was sent to do. "Driver, please take me to the nearest motel instead."

After he'd settled into an unpretentious motel, it was time for lunch and he never missed that. He strolled along Main Street looking at signs and decided on pizza. He stepped into a small café called Whaler's Pizza. It smelled divine. They served customers at the take-out counter or one could eat at one of their small tables near the back door.

"I'd like a Whopper Pizza, please, with pepperoni and sausage, extra cheese, broccoli and mushrooms," he said. "Oh, by the way, do you have an extra ingredient that you could add to surprise me?" W.D. liked to get his money's worth.

The young woman smiled at him and said, "Why yes, we can put some sprouts on there for you."

"Okay, do it. Hmm, I also need a glass of ice cold milk." He turned and headed for a small table. As he sat down to wait, he looked around. He was surprised to see a nice-looking man at a nearby table with a cane.

Now that's odd, he thought. He looks like an athlete, so muscular, tan and fit looking.

"Howdy," said W.D. looking at the man sympathetically, "Did you have an accident?"

He was taken aback by the blue of the man's eyes as they rested on him rather aggressively. He did not answer.

W.D. wondered who he was. The silence was uncomfortable and W.D. wasn't sure if he should proceed with his friendly banter.

"Your pizza's ready, sir."

W.D. went back to the counter, paid the bill, tipped his usual 12.5 percent, and took the tray back to the table. He tucked his napkin around the collar of his plaid Bemidji Woolen Mills cotton shirt and concentrated on every bite of his delicious pizza.

After about 20 minutes he heard the scrape of a chair as the young man pushed away from his table and stood up. Leaning on his cane, he thumped his way over to W.D.'s table.

"Say, you're not from around here, are you?" The young man frowned at W.D.

"No sir, I'm not. My name is W.D. Caldwell, and I'm a technician with CBS Television in L.A. and I'm here scouting out locations for a documentary we're shootin' here."

As he leaned into W.D.'s table, the young man cried out in pain. W.D. glanced down at his legs to see what was wrong.

"Oh, son, hurt your leg?"

"No, no, I just had a sad reminder of that city...*Los Angeles or Lost Angels.*"

"Oh, my goodness," said W.D., "Why?"

"Well, it's my accident. It was caused by a woman who left me to live in L.A."

W.D. looked at him closely. "Glad you survived, son. My word, how'd that happen. Did she mean to hurt you?"

"Ah, yeah, it seems like yesterday, but it was over a year ago." He reflected a bit and continued, "Yes and no. She just dumped me and then-er-the accident happened." He looked away. "I've got pins in my legs, arms, hands, and head. I had a cast on my neck and ribs, and it's been slow healing…but the doctors say I'll make a complete recovery."

"Well, it must have helped that you were in such good physical shape," said W.D. The young man did not reply. "What's your name, son? Mine is W.D. Caldwell," He decided not to try and shake hands, "Do you live around here?"

"Glad to meet you, W.D., just call me Randall." He stared at W.D. with his icy blue eyes. "I live over in Springs."

"What kind of work do you do…Randall?" W.D. tried to be noncommittal, "I'm lookin' for kind of an assistant in this area to help me out with some research. I need to find out all I can about a local author named Aldean Matheson, who supposedly lived in or still lives out in Montauk."

"I know him and–ah–where he lives. In fact, I worked for him. I built his deck and repaired his dock out in Montauk. There's no one I don't know…being in construction like I was."

"Good. You're hired, son." W.D. was surprised to find a local informant so fast. One who'd even worked for Matheson. "Would a thousand bucks take care of your services?"

"Agreed, old man." Randall broke into a cunning smile. He sat down and rested his cane.

22

"I was in the right place, but it musta been the wrong time" blared out over the radio of Randall's old Ford F-150 truck. W.D. was at the wheel and they were singing along with Dr. John, as they sped down the Old Montauk Highway. They were keeping time with the music, bouncing up and down, with no springs to spare their rear ends, heading to Gurney's Inn.

Randall stopped singing, a look of wonder on his face, as W.D. passed a big semi while riding the clutch. "Jeez, you sure know how to drive, old man."

"Yeah, you got that right, son," said W.D., as he thought longingly of his muscle car back home. He wondered if he'd ever make it back to race at the Bemidji Speedway. He stepped it down so he was now doing 80 miles an hour; cannon balling down the straightaway like a bat out of hell.

"I've reserved a room for you at Gurney's for the next few days," said W.D., "I'm gonna stay there tonight, but then I'm going to camp out on the beach at the East Loop Campsite."

Randall was desperately grasping at his seat belt, his nerves frayed, but still trying to remain cool. "Yeah – okey-dokey I guess. But, ah, what is it that you want me to do?"

"Uh, well, help me figure out what Aldean is up to. You know him, you worked for him. I'll pick you up during the day and we'll go fishing or some damn thing, while watching the cottage." W.D. kept his eyes on the road. "But, I intend to do a creepy crawl to get closer to the cottage so I can get a good look at Matheson in his lair – you know get some photos."

"Hey, wait a minute here. You know how to creepy crawl?"

"Oh, yeah, CBS made a documentary about secret agents. I learned by watching them."

"Have you got a low-light camera with you?" Randall was getting pretty excited about the upcoming activities.

"Yup," said W.D., "part of my job, finding locations." He slowed down as they neared the lights of Montauk.

Randall suddenly became serious. "Say, old man, turn off at the next rest stop and park. Let me tell you what I know about Aldean from workin' for him – you know – personal stuff."

"Okay, son," said W.D., "the more I know about him, his habits, er, lifestyle, the better it will be to sum up his activities in Los Angeles."

"Hunh? What do you mean activities in L.A.? I thought you were researching locations for a documentary?"

"Well yes, but it's actually based on Aldean's script. CBS Studios bought the rights to it." He pulled off the road and cut the motor. He didn't answer the question.

Randall leaned back against the seat, relaxing after his hair-raising ride, and ready to earn his fee. "Uh, Aldean is a serious writer, he writes every day, and he has kind of a writer's den. He checks references and makes calls to experts. I've heard him ask questions. He really grills 'em. He has a tape recorder on his phone and turns it on as he's talking. Later, his assistant Stella will type up a rough transcript from the audio cassette."

Randall drew in his breath as if remembering something.

Then he got a wry look on his face. "But Aldean loves women too much; he can't seem to help himself. He has more than one relationship going on at a time. It gets to be a ticking time bomb."

"Hmmm, yeah, I can imagine," said W.D.

Randall doubted that, but he continued: "Uh, Aldean likes to write naked – you know – no clothes on and that can create problems. He takes breaks and heads out to the beach. He's been picked up crossing the highway to the beach by both the New York State Police and the Easthampton Police and cited for lewd behavior and being a public nuisance."

"I wonder how he gets away with such eccentric behavior."

Randall shook his head. "Well, he's pretty famous. And rich, too. One of the worst things about him is his stutter. When he gets excited he just has a meltdown. He's on medication for his speech problem, but the pills raise his libido."

"Good God. Sounds like the pills make the problem worse. Has he spent any time in jail?"

"Oh, yeah, but it's been hushed up."

#   #   #

The next morning they set out for Hither Hills State Park. W.D. arranged the three-day pass and received a sticker and a permit. He put up the small tent on a concrete slab near a picnic table. After everything was in order, he pulled a Hamm's beer out of the cooler and offered one to Randall. "No, thanks, old man. Stopped drinking awhile back."

While W.D. got the fishing rods ready they enjoyed the rhythmic sound of the ocean, the soaring sea gulls, and the beauty of the sunny rays that magnified the landscape into

Technicolor. W.D. had never seen anything like it. No wonder someone who could live anywhere in the world would choose to live here.

They surfcasted most of the day and Randall caught a striped bass in the late afternoon. W.D. noticed that he handled himself adroitly; he didn't use his cane once and didn't seem to be as crippled as he pretended.

"Hey, good job, Randall. It's a nice one. I'll take care of cleaning and filleting." W.D. had started a small fire in the grill and began work on their supper.

"I'm going to take the truck out for a spin on the beach while you get our food ready," said Randall "Thanks for taking care of everything." He was soon off, the radio turned up, driving like crazy through the sand.

W.D. was really enjoying himself, too. He washed off the fillets, shook them in a little baggie full of spices, and laid them down carefully into the really hot cast iron skillet slicked with some vegetable oil. He heard them crackle and smelled the outdoor smoky aroma that made his mouth water. He then opened up a can of baked beans, put some tin foil over the top and set it on the grill, along with a pan of baking powder biscuits. He heard the truck before he saw it and knew Randall was back. "Hey, did you have a nice ride?" He looked over at Randall who was holding a small piece of paper. "Yeah, I saw a girl on the beach, gave her a ride, and got her number."

"Yeah, hmm. Didn't tell her anything, did you?" W.D. gave him a stare. Crikey, that Randall must be a magnet for women.

"Nah," he said as he plated up their supper and dug in. "Golly, old man, this is delicious – there is no end to your talents."

"Well, heh heh, no guess not – ah, this sure looks mighty good," "he said. He asked for God's blessings on their meal, and then dug in, too. Sated, they sat back on their camp chairs and looked out over the ocean, enjoying the evening: W.D. with a bottle of beer in his hand, and Randall with a Coke.

The sun was going down and a light breeze was coming up. "I'm going to take you back to Gurney's before it gets too dark." Randall had cited his injuries as being too painful to sleep outdoors so W.D. had him stay at the resort.

"Yeah. Okay. What time do you want to pick me up tomorrow, then?"

"Oh, around nine, same place I picked you up this morning." After W.D. washed up and put out the campfire, they headed for the truck and the drive over to the Inn.

# # #

After W.D. dropped off Randall he headed back to the campsite. The sun had gone down and there was a lazy feeling in the air. He thought about calling Christian at the L.A. office tonight but then decided to wait until he had something to report. He looked over at Aldean's beachfront home through binoculars. It was pretty basic, one end was a slant roof, and the center was lower and looked like an add-on. He knew it sat on two expensive acres, but it looked like a typical workman's cottage, complete with barbeque. He had checked the property earlier but there had been no activity during the day, one car arrived around noon and left an hour later. He could hear a dog barking, but never saw one. He carefully considered his plans for the early morning hours and then fell asleep in the camp chair. He awakened at around 2:00 a.m. and decided it was time to head over to Aldean's cottage.

He pulled on a black tee shirt over his blue jeans, grabbed the black nylon jacket with extra pockets for the camera, flashlight, packet of gum, and a flare. On second thought, he also picked up the mace can and an I.D. card identifying him as a private investigator with the Handler Agency in Malibu.

He started out walking, determined the distance, and then he fell to his knees and started to crawl. After crawling, stopping, crawling, then resting, W.D. came within view of the cottage. He was surprised to hear arguing in the darkened house. A woman started screaming and then the lights went on. He thought he heard a gunshot. He remained in a low crouch, watching what was about to happen: The front door opened and a little Jack Russell Terrier ran out, barking and leaping about. Right behind the dog was a slender, dark-skinned woman carrying a large metal box and a small shovel. Her long black hair was hanging in her eyes and she seemed like she was in a trance, just standing there, not moving, and staring at a spot.

Finally she started to dig, turning over the earth quickly without regard to where it went. After twenty minutes she had a created a sizeable hole in the ground. W.D. watched as she placed the box in the hole. She quickly covered up the burial site, laid the shovel down, and called for the dog. "Here Prince, c'mon boy."

He didn't obey her. She ran around the cottage in a frenzy, calling for the dog. She finally found him near the beach and carried him back, crooning in relief.

The woman with the dog rushed into the house and slammed the door. All the lights stayed on for about ten minutes then everything went dark. W.D. slithered around the cottage; he didn't know what to make of this. He got a low-light photo of the hole now covered with dirt and round 3:30 a. m., he left the area. He did a creepy crawl back to the tent, stood outside for awhile, looking up at the stars trying to process what he'd just seen. He brushed his teeth and crawled into his bedroll with his clothes on.

Around 4:30 a.m. he awakened to the smell of smoke. Almost simultaneously he heard the screaming sirens. He jumped up quickly when he realized there must be a fire nearby. Was it one of his fellow campers? Went to sleep with a lighted cigarette? He shoved all his gear back into his pockets and headed out to the beachfront. Then he saw that the fire and smoke was coming from Aldean's cottage.

It must have started earlier, perhaps shortly after he'd left the scene, because the cottage was now fully engulfed in flames. The firefighters had arrived and W.D. ran up the hill to get a better look. He saw the Montauk and Springs fire departments, an ambulance, as well as the East Hampton Police car all parked in a semi-circle. He was planning to move in closer when he heard an explosion that caused so much thick black smoke that he had to leave the area so he wouldn't suffocate. He returned to his camp site near the beachfront, really glad that the breezes were blowing the smoke out to sea to the north.

"Hey, old man, what just happened?" Randall was standing near the tent, leaning on his cane, staring over at the cottage.

"Good God – you gave me a start – how'd you get out here?" W.D. was shocked to see him.

"Ah, I talked a tourist into bringing me out here," Randall looked down. "You know, when I heard the fire trucks go past the Inn, well, I thought maybe you were in trouble."

"Hmm, well glad you got here." W.D. didn't buy the tourist fib, he figured that Randall met some woman, perhaps in the lobby of the hotel, and she'd brought him out.

"You know, I'm very surprised about the fire." W.D. wiped his eyes from the effects of the smoke, "I wonder what really happened – there was an explosion a few minutes ago. Could it be arson?"

Randall and W.D. decided to take a walk over to the cottage a little after 5:00. They became part of a gaggle of neighbors and tourists who were curious about the catastrophe in their midst. They saw paramedics had retrieved a body prior to the explosion and were loading it into an ambulance. They shut the doors, backed up, and sped off. A sigh went up through the crowd and murmurs of 'was that Aldean?' floated through the air as if on a radio wave.

"I'm going over there and hang out a little bit." W.D. clutched his I.D. card and made his way, leaving Randall in a cluster of people. He did a quick scan of the area around the cottage, but did not see the woman or the dog. He wondered if they were still inside, burnt to a cinder.

"Say, Officer, I'm W.D. Caldwell, ah, here's my card. I wondered if you could tell me what happened here."

"No sir, we can't. But as you probably surmised there's been a fatality – the owner of the property – luckily we got the body out before the explosion." The officer handed W.D.'s card back without comment and seemed in shock as he shook his head and said, "You know, he was a world-famous author – we don't know what happened here."

W.D. was nodding his head in agreement when he was shoved aside by a man in fire gear who said, "I'm with the Suffolk County Arson Squad – when will we be able to access the house?"

The officer looked over his shoulder and said, "My guess is early this afternoon – there are still some hot spots."

W.D. backed away concerned that he might be questioned as to what he was doing there. He slipped back into the crowd; careful to stand behind Randall.

"Let's get out of here. Aldean's dead, and the arson squad just arrived." They slowly made their way back to the beach so as to not create attention. They got into the truck, W.D. at the wheel, and decided to go back to Randall's room at Gurney's and watch the news of the fire on television.

W.D. planned to call Chris Handler that evening to report the suspicious death of Matheson and the strange circumstance of the long-haired woman burying a metal box in his backyard just before the house burned down. He wondered if Aldean wasn't the perfect example of being *in the wrong place at the wrong time.*

23

Things happened pretty fast after the fire cooled and W.D. decided to take action that very night. He called Handler who was quick to point out that W.D. should call the East Hampton Police and report what he'd seen.

An officer called back immediately and set up an appointment for W.D. to accompany Detective Marlon Samuels to the scene of the fire. Aldean's death had been big news on the major networks and a topic of conversation among people at the Inn and throughout Montauk. How did it happen? Why did his cottage burn down? Was it arson?

W.D. waited for the detective in the lobby of Gurney's Inn. Soon he saw the officer he'd approached that morning at the scene of the fire. "Good evening, Detective Samuels, I understand I'll be joining you tonight."

"Yes, good to meet you, again, Mr. Caldwell. We got your call to retrieve some possible buried evidence as witnessed by you, ah, while on surveillance, I believe?"

W.D. turned away quickly as he did not want to get into any detail. "Yes, sir, that's correct."

They decided to drive the unmarked 1980 black Mercedes Benz E Class and proceeded to the gate leading to the main beach. As Samuels pulled up onto the beach, the sand was still firm. It would be low tide until 2:54 A.M., but then high tide would make it difficult to get back. After checking the tide table for Fort Pond Bay, W.D determined that they had two hours before they'd have to vamoose. They pulled up near his old campsite and smelled the acrid smoke residue in the air. It was strangely quiet, there were no night birds or small animals around; they'd fled the scene, too.

They got out of the car and W.D. suited up in his all-weather jacket and rubber boots. His Ruger was in a leather holster around his waist designed for a quick draw. He carried a flashlight, a low light camera around his neck, and a small shovel under his arm. In his pocket he had garbage bags, a pair of gloves and his ubiquitous Juicy Fruit Gum. Samuels was wearing a long duster-type windbreaker with a Filson All Weather hat and gloves. They took off walking, crossing the road, carefully ambling across the meadow, ducking low when headlights appeared. They circled the house or what was left of it, flashing the light on the scorched trees. As he looked around W.D. had sad feelings: "*God, what a shame, he had so much to live for.*" Aldean's death seemed so wrong; happening so unexpectedly! Was it really an accident?

They said very little as W.D. headed straight for the burial site just making out a faint outline around the hole dug by the woman. He didn't know what to expect. Could be just dog bones for all he knew. Maybe Prince's Christmas present. He wondered what the East Hampton Police detective would do in that case?

W.D.'s flashlight was attached to a stand and illuminated the area. He started digging and was surprised by the loose dirt – how easy it was to move. But then he realized that it had been only a matter of hours since the metal box was buried there. It was deeper than he first thought and he felt he had to take a break. He turned off the flashlight, and took out a stick of gum, offered one to Samuels. He declined, but W.D. paused a few minutes savoring the taste. Soon he was ready to finish the job.

He hit something hard and it made a ringing sound. It was the metal box with a snap lid like a cashbox. He guessed it was locked and gave a quick thought as to how to open it. But after he lifted it out, he saw that it had no lock. He got excited thinking about what he might find, took a deep breath, and lifted the lid.

He stared at a silver Smith & Wesson semi-automatic pistol, then reached beneath it and saw what looked like a hotel bill, and at the bottom a few typed sheets stapled together like a legal document. They took photos of the stuff in the box; put it back in the hole, and took a few more. W.D. reached in a second time and took it all out, put it securely in the garbage bag, and tied a knot at the top, handing it to Samuels in a chain of custody. He quickly refilled the empty hole. He stared down at it – what the hell was that gun all about?

He gathered his equipment, scraped the dirt off the shovel, and both men dusted off their clothes, then walked quickly back to the car. W.D. was glad to have had such a quick retrieval. He'd never met a man as tight-lipped as Detective Samuels who did not waste energy on superfluous motion as he carefully placed the evidence bag on the front seat, before getting into the driver's side. W.D. jumped into the passenger seat with the package between them.

Suddenly he was aware of another vehicle, its headlights bouncing up and down, coming straight at them. Samuels switched on the brights and hit the spotlight. The other vehicle slowed down. Jeez what was going on here? As he got closer he saw it was a small, open Jeep 4WD with a long-haired woman at the wheel. Samuels honked the horn and only then did the vehicle stop to let them pass. But she didn't wave or acknowledge them in any way; and the detective drove on – in no mood to confront.

Back at Gurney's, W.D. was dropped off near the lobby entrance. It was time to call Chris Handler again to tell him about the evening. He felt a rising sense of excitement. Why were these items buried outside Aldean's home shortly before he died in the fire? One thing he was sure of: he was the only eye witness who'd seen the woman bury the stuff. Well, not exactly. What about the woman herself?

He bet she knew why she buried that box. Had he met her just now on her way back to dig it up? He smiled when he thought of the gangbuster tizzy she'd have when she found out the metal box was gone.

24

Monday morning W.D. joined Randall for breakfast. He'd already ordered a stack of pancakes with bacon and eggs and was busy looking around the room. After W.D. ordered a cinnamon roll and a big pot of dark roast coffee, he opened up the morning newspaper.

"Huh. There's that lady I met on the beach the other day. I gave her and the dog a ride."

"Ah, who?" W.D. looked around.

"That one," Randall nodded in the direction of a woman across the room. "Isn't she gorgeous – all that long black hair? Her name is Joyce…something to do with the wind."

W.D spotted her. She was biting into a croissant and he recognized her as the woman, who'd been outside Aldean Matheson's house the night of the fire; the one who'd buried the metal box with the gun in it. He realized he was looking at Joyce Santa Anna.

W.D. stood up and without a word, left the room. He had to make an urgent call to Handler. He used his special phone outside Gurney's to call him. "Hey, Chris, it's W.D. here. Just spotted Joyce Santa Anna here at Gurney's Inn. Yup. She's eating breakfast. Okay, I can do that. Do you want me to call the East Hampton Police? Okay. Yeah. Sure. Over and out."

W.D. leaned against a wall for a moment considering his next step. Handler had told him to make a Citizen's Arrest and to hold her there until the East Hampton Police arrived. W.D. thought about his Ruger. Did he need it? Would she pull a weapon on him?

He decided to go up to his room and get his gun. He called Gurney's Security and talked to the guard who said he could assist in the arrest. They met in the lobby. Alphonso was a small man with a large moustache who said he'd just had a call from the police and they were on their way. He wanted to know what the woman had done. Was she dangerous? He looked thrilled to have a role to play.

"Ah, she's a person of interest in a criminal investigation," said W.D., "the police want to talk to her. Let's hold her in the lobby until they arrive."

"Okay, man," he said as he picked up a phone call from the hotel manager.

"Yes, sir that is correct. We are proceeding to the breakfast room now. Yes, I put up a sign that the lobby was closed."

They strode into the breakfast room and over to the black-haired woman's chair.

"Ms. Joyce Santa Anna?"

"Yes, what is it? We've already ordered," she looked up at W.D. with a smirk, "but we could use some more coffee."

"Ms. Santa Anna, I am making a Citizen's Arrest. Please accompany me to the lobby."

"What in God's name are you talking about, you old fart? You can't arrest me. I haven't done anything."

"You can make a scene or not. The police are on their way. They want to talk to you," he shifted his eyes to Alphonso, "I have hotel security with me and we are both armed. Please, step out to the lobby now, ma'am."

Alphonso moved closer and gently touched his snapped holster. He looked at W.D and nodded in agreement.

Joyce stood up and then looked over at the other diners, smiled, and shook her hair back over her shoulders.

"I'm getting so famous – I'll be back in just a few minutes, have to clear up a few things." She turned and breezed out of the room, with W.D. and Alphonso right behind her.

# # #

Randall, who'd just finished breakfast, was bug-eyed with disbelief as he watched the scenario unfold across the room.

"My God, what's that old man up to?" He wiped his mouth with a linen napkin, got up and hurried out to the lobby.

An officer was reading Santa Anna her Miranda Rights. Then they escorted her out to the police car for the ride to the station. Randall saw that W.D. was arguing with one of the policemen. Then he heard the officer say in a final tone, "We'll call you, sir, when and if we need you. Good day."

Randall stood there out of sight and waited until the squad car left the hotel, then he went up to W.D. and touched him lightly on the shoulder.

"Hey, old man, what are you doin'?"

"Oh, hi, well, my boss asked me to make a Citizen's Arrest of the female friend of Aldean Matheson's. It seems she's a person of interest."

"Ohhh, really!"

"Yeah, she was allegedly with him before he died in the fire."

"Good God…is that right? She told me she was staying here at the Inn on vacation in a cabin for pet owners."

"Huh, do you know the number of the cabin?" W.D. looked very concerned, "We'd better check on that little dog."

"Oh, yeah, it's # 302 – just down the beach."

"Okay, let's go."

They found the door open and the maid was vacuuming the living room. She had the dog locked in the bathroom and he was barking his head off, scratching the door, and seriously whining. The maid looked over at W.D. with concern in her eyes, "You know that lady with long hair, she mean to that little dog."

W.D. opened the bathroom door, knelt down, and said, "Oh, it's okay, Prince, everything will be all right, little guy."

The dog wagged his little stubby tail and licked W.D.'s hand. His little nose quivered. He knew he'd found a friend. W.D. thought he'd never seen a cuter dog: all white with black ears and a big round brown patch over his right eye. He looked closer and saw the swollen lid and blood drops on his fur. It was plain that this was a dog that was going to need his protection.

"Wow! W.D. how'd you know his name?"

"Oh, I didn't. You know, just a guess."

"Hmm, wonder what kind of dog he is?"

"I'd say a purebred Jack Russell Terrier. Perhaps three years old," said W.D. who turned to look at Randall. "That reminds me, you will need to go get him some dog food – 15 cans of Caesare for purebreds and 2 boxes of puppy pads."

"Awww, W.D. I ain't goin' to go shoppin' for no dog."

"Let me tell you something, son, you've done very little to earn the fee we agreed upon. I paid you half in advance. You've run up a tremendous bill here at Gurney's – what with your soda pop, your movies, room service, and Spa bill all charged to me. So, unless you cooperate with me and go get that dog food, it will remain unpaid by me and I might mention, so will the other half of your retainer. So God damn it – move it and I mean right now."

Randall was chagrined; he turned quickly and headed out the door. "Jeez. Okay, I'm off to get the freakin' dog food and puppy pads."

W.D. wanted him out of there because he planned to shakedown the premises. When the maid left discreetly, closing the door quietly, he slipped on his gloves. He began working quickly; checking the bedroom, the closets, and then the front room and the desk. It was only when he opened a briefcase that he found some interesting information: the return portion of a flight to California, a passport, a one-way open ticket to Paris, France, and a legal document that looked like a will prepared by an attorney from New York City. He studied the passport with interest: the name was Jyaana Shakti Densmore, 33 years old, with an Oxnard, California address.

He put the briefcase in a garbage bag, along with the dog leash, and a box of dog kibbles and with Prince under his jacket, headed back to his room. As soon as he shut and locked the hotel room door, he called Handler and gave him a full report. Handler was pleased but told W.D. to return everything to the cabin, except the dog. He suggested taking photos of the contents in the briefcase and the dog's bruises and then call the East Hampton Police to report the evidence in the cabin.

Prince started barking and running around the room as W.D. concluded their conversation. He heard Handler laughing as he hung up. He was glad Handler seemingly agreed to his taking the dog. He set out a bowl of fresh water and poured the kibbles into a big ash tray. After Prince devoured everything, he took him out for a run on the beach.

Then he went to work. He took photos of the documents and walked everything back to Joyce's cabin and then called the police. When he returned to his room he started to pack. He called the airlines to add Prince to his ticket, paid the extra charges, and arranged for the car service to pick him up in the morning for the ride to the Long Island MacArthur Airport with a quick stop at a vet's to get a health certificate for Prince.

Later that evening, Randall brought over the right dog food and puppy pads. He asked the front desk to deliver the large bag to W.D.'s room. He knew everything the old man said was true and he felt a little ashamed for earning such easy money. But he only felt a twinge for a few seconds.

25

Chris Handler was back at CBS Monday afternoon to interview Tarintina's research team. Since Wade was not back in the office yet, the staff seemed uncertain how to proceed. They seemed off-kilter. There were starts, stops, and delays, in their answers. They were all originally hired to work on a documentary about an illegal marijuana growing operation in the Shasta-Trinity National Forest. But due to the death of two unsuspecting tourists who stumbled onto the garden, the documentary was temporarily shelved. One thing was for certain: all of the researchers were experienced and had worked for other production companies, either in movies or for television. Well, except for one: Dyanna Dahlberg. She'd come from the CBS Public Relations in New York City.

He decided to interview one employee twice. His name was Gervaise Hallaway and he yielded a tip that changed everything. Initially Gervaise told Handler that Wade put the brakes on the marijuana documentary because law enforcement had an ongoing investigation. In the second interview, Gervaise told Handler more about Aldean Matheson who'd written the book about the illegal marijuana gardens and the disagreement that blew up over the option renewal payment from Wade. Gervaise said that Matheson thought CBS has ripped him off and had threatened to kill Wade. He filed a lawsuit against CBS to stop production. He then asked Gervaise about Dyanna. What was her role in the research department? Gervaise said he didn't know other than she was enthusiastic and didn't mind staying late.

After bidding everyone goodnight, Handler waited for his driver in the CBS parking lot. Within ten minutes, the Wrangler pulled up and David stepped out, opened the door for Handler to get in the back, and then turned and got back into the driver's seat.

"Good evening, Boss, hope it was a productive day," said David who looked over his shoulder quickly before they sped off.

"Why yes, it was." But Handler looked perplexed as he thought of how odd it was that Sarah, another researcher, told him that they'd started work on a documentary about Indian casinos, based on another book by Aldean Matheson. He leaned back in his seat and mentally tabulated the huge cost of switching television projects in midstream, finding new advertisers to fund them, and then paying Matheson an option payment for another book? While he still had a law suit against them for the first one?

The next morning, Handler called Dyanna at CBS. "This is Chris Handler. I wonder if I might make arrangements to interview you. I have some questions about why you were hired at CBS?"

"Oh, Chris, yes, of course, I would have no problem with that. When would you like to see me?"

"Dyanna, I'd like to interview you this afternoon, if you don't mind. Perhaps you could have a late lunch with me? I could pick you up at your residence around five if that's convenient?"

"Oh, yes it is. I believe you have my home address. I will see you this afternoon."

Chris made reservations at Spago's for 6:00. He was well known there and got an immediate booking.

# # #

It was just five when the Jeep Wrangler pulled up at the front entrance of Dyanna's Mulholland Drive condo. The doorman greeted Chris Handler who indicated he was there to pick up Ms. Dahlberg.

"Mr. Handler, please take the first elevator up to the fourth floor." As Chris stepped off the elevator into a foyer, he was greeted by Dyanna and two elderly women who were smiling at him and seemed rather anxious to say hello.

"Chris, this is my Mother Gunhilde Dahlberg and my Aunt Anita Sorenson. They are visiting me from McIntosh, Minnesota."

"It's wonderful to meet you, Chris," they chorused.

"My pleasure," he said as he smiled at one, then the other. He thought they were adorable. He bowed and kissed their hands, as Dyanna quickly shrugged into her coat. They slipped out the door, and headed for the elevator. As they rode down to the lobby, she was struck again by his handsome visage and his old world charm.

David, the driver, stepped out of the Jeep parked in front of the door and escorted Dyanna into the backseat, and then Chris. "Good evening, Madam, it's a lovely night, isn't it?" They pulled away carefully from the curb and set out for the restaurant on Sunset Strip. Dyanna was surprised by the Jeep; she had fully expected a limousine. But then, how many private investigators did she know?

"Dyanna, I am so glad you could meet with me today. I'm afraid I'm going to have to mix a little business in with the pleasure of your company. I have some questions that have come up since I saw you at CBS."

After entering Spago's through the back door, the *maitre de'* escorted them to a table on the second floor, where they were seated next to a large plant for privacy. There was a fun-charged vibration in the air as Chris ordered the classic Spago Pizza with Caviar and a bottle of red wine from Napa Valley. They chatted about their day and a little bit about their professions while enjoying the delicious pizza and the accompanying red wine. Soon it was time for dessert and coffee and Chris looked expectantly at Dyanna.

"I am curious to know how you came to be hired by the CBS Documentary Department without the requisite background in film and script writing."

"I know, Chris, that's true and it puzzles me greatly, too. To give you a little history – ! was the Vice President of Public Relations for CBS in New York City for four years. When I felt it was time for a change I contacted Ted Jameson, here in the CBS Promotion Department, about a transfer. I have a graphic design background and it would have been a good fit for me. He came to New York City, interviewed me, and told me he was seriously interested in hiring me." Dyanna took a sip of her wine while she determined how detailed she should get. "Well, briefly, I took my vacation and some extra time off and waited to hear from Jameson. While on vacation I went ahead and bought some property in northwestern Minnesota, as an investment – ah, it's where my family is from."

"Did Jameson bring you to Los Angeles for an additional interview?"

"Yes, he did. He flew me to Los Angeles, all expenses

paid, for an additional interview. I returned to Minnesota after three days without a job offer. About three weeks later, Jameson called and said I was hired and to get ready to start work in about a month."

"Did you start work in the CBS Promotion Department?"

"No. That was the strange part. I arrived in LA and did not go to work for around four weeks. But during that time I was put up in a hotel and had appointments with an agent who had been hired to write a contract for me. I was shown various apartments and finally settled on a condo on Mulholland Drive. Finally I arrived at CBS only to find out I was assigned to the News and Documentary Department and was to report to Wade Tarintina, a producer and former radio personality, whom I'd never met."

"Did he explain to you why you were shifted from one job to another? One department to another? Sounds highly irregular, you know."

"No, he didn't ever explain. I guess I thought he would eventually. What was also strange is that my salary was upped in the contract and the duration was extended to five years with an option to renew. But even stranger yet, Chris," she hesitated, "Tarintina told me he didn't hire me. The new CEO Mr. Walberg did, sight unseen."

"Hmmm. I would like to read your contract. Something is very, very odd here."

"Yes, Chris, it is very odd. I met the author in question-Aldean Matheson when I was employed at the New York station. I was dating a local man who worked for Matheson and I had a brief introduction to him. We did not exchange cards or ever contact each other. I will be glad to answer any questions about this visit."

Handler was not surprised that she'd met him. He decided to call it a night. Her recollection may bring some insight into the Matheson persona and help Chris understand why Tarintina was almost murdered. Sometimes information came from the strangest source.

26

It was hard for me to fall asleep. I was so stimulated by my evening at Spago's with Chris Handler. The lunch was supposedly a pretext for additional questions regarding the assault on my boss, Wade Tarintina. Chris's questioning of me was careful, but I knew he was looking for reasons from the staff interviews about what the motive might have been. I'd met Aldean Matheson some years before. It was my last date with Randall Lester, a man I had to file a restraining order on.

I was living part-time in Sag Harbor and dating him. We'd arranged a date for a late summer night in July. He suggested we drive to Gurney's Inn in Montauk and have dinner on the patio overlooking the beach. He had the top down on his Mustang. He opened my door, sat me down, and kissed the top of my head, and we took off, my hair flying every which way. We were in a good mood.

Randall surprised me at Gurney's when he jerked up with a quick motion from the wicker chair and said, "Say, let's go visit Aldean Matheson, the famous writer-he lives just down the beach in a cottage. Dyanna, you'd get a kick out of him."

"Ah, how do you know him, Randall?"

"I work for him-or I should say, I used to work for him. I built his deck and wooden garden fence." He raised an eyebrow and said, "He's really different."

"Oh, in what way?"

"Well, he's unconventional-very rich, but acts poor. He's a womanizer, without being good-looking. Oh, God, guess I can't nail down his appeal."

"Humph, doesn't sound like anyone I'd want to meet," I said.

"Yeah, well, I still think you would. His books are best sellers and they are supposedly very well written and researched. He himself has lived with what he calls indigenous people. He makes a big deal of being an environmental activist."

"Does that mean he joins walks for peace and protests? Joins marches and sit-ins? Makes speeches to rabble rousing groups?"

"Yeah, yeah, that's right. But lately, he's been spending time in Hollywood-they 've optioned several of his books for movies and television documentaries."

"Okay, let's drop in. You don't think he'd mind, do you?"

"Not at all! He likes to meet beautiful women any time of the day or night."

We left Gurney's and drove a mile or so further down the Montauk Highway, parked at a rest stop, and then walked over the grass to the back door. We could see the lights on inside the cottage and as we got closer, we heard soft music playing.

Randall knocked and I held my breath. Was I about to meet a long-haired, irascible writer with lust in his eyes?

"Come in," called a female voice. We stepped into a lovely domestic scene of a couple playing backgammon, a bottle of uncorked white wine near the lamp, and a big yellow cat asleep on the back of an overstuffed chair.

"Hey, Randall – so good to see you. Please join us," said Aldean.

"Oh, Aldean, this is my girlfriend, Dyanna Dahlberg, she's a TV executive from New York City. We were just over at Gurney's for dinner and thought we'd stop in. How's everything going?"

"Well. Pretty good. B-b-b-been spending time m Los Angeles. Good to meet you, Dyanna. Ah, this is Lynette Larson, my girlfriend-she's b-b-been beating me a-a-a-all to hell." He smiled lovingly at her.

Lynette stood up, poured two glasses of white wine, and pulled over two chairs for us to sit near them.

"Randall, I've moved in with Aldean since you last worked here." Her face was glowing with happiness. I saw that she was a large young woman with vibrant blonde hair. Not a great beauty, but striking.

"Congrats," said Randall, with a kooky smile on his face.

She looked at us, and then came closer, examining us. "You know, you two look alike. You should get married."

We laughed and Randall made an off-the-cuff comment about that being the secret of a happy marriage.

Aldean stood up and motioned for me to follow him. "Dyanna, I'd like to show you my writing studio." I noticed that he had a large nose, a receding hairline, and was around six feet tall.

I agreed and followed him up a couple of steps into an enclosed porch-like structure. It had two desks, each with an electric typewriter on it, two telephones, a tape recorder and a pile of books on the floor.

"I have an assistant who helps me with my research,"

he said as he pointed to the white walls. I stared at them. They were covered with diagrams, notes made to himself, money deposited in the bank, and scribbled reminders of social events long past. Strangely enough there was also an outline of an oil pipeline sketched on the opposite wall and a big wobbly sign, "Stop Fracking."

"Aldean, why do you write directly on your walls?"

"Oh," he said, "prisoners do it."

I had no response to that.

Then I noticed a framed photo of a beautiful dark-skinned woman with long hair on his cluttered desk.

"Aldean, who is this? Your daughter?"

"N-n-n-n-oooo, she's the love of my life. We have a deep spiritual t-t-t-tie."

I didn't get a chance to question him before Lynette called out: "Aldean, ready to go out for our walk?"

He grabbed a light sweater from the back of the door and turned toward us, "Hey, why don't you two join us?"

I looked at Randall and he smiled, "Sure, why not?" We took off our shoes and followed them to the beach, the stars lighting our way.

Suddenly Aldean stopped and pushed Lynnette away from him. "No, you're not. I'm b-b-b-breaking up with you tonight," he said with no warning.

She stood stock still, and then started to cry. Soon it escalated until she was hysterical. But Aldean did not move, did not explain, or console her. He ignored us.

I motioned to Randall that we should leave immediately. When I looked back, I saw she was still crying and Aldean had not moved.

The ride back to Sag Harbor was quiet. Suddenly as we neared my home, Randall said, "I knew he'd do that. I couldn't believe he'd invited her to live with him."

"Oh, really!" I was surprised. "Why did you think that? They seemed so compatible."

"Yeah and they are. But Lynette whispered to me that Joyce Santa Anna had been calling to say she wanted to move to Montauk to live with Aldean."

"Hmmm, so he's kicking Lynette out?"

"Yes, that's exactly what I'm saying. Sorry you had to see their dysfunctional relationship – him and his women."

After we said goodnight I stood by my back door and thought about the photograph of the beautiful woman I'd seen on Aldean's desk. Yes, she certainly looked like trouble.

The next day I told all I knew to Handler including my impression of the beautiful woman in the photograph- Joyce Santa Anna.

27

Marlon Samuels always enjoyed coming home to Sag Harbor. No matter what kind of day he'd had at the station, he felt relaxation pulse through his entire body as he turned into the dirt driveway and parked in a spot near the kitchen door.

He thought his wife Avis had done a fantastic job of decorating their home. He especially liked the old-fashioned tieback curtains along with the plants and herbs growing in small pots in the windows. They'd combined the dining and kitchen areas so that he and his son could watch Avis cook as she was a Ritz-Escoffier graduate with a flair for timing.

Just as he came in the doorway his wife was putting a large Quiche Lorraine into the convection oven. French Escargot was baking in the gas range oven, and a large triple washed head of lettuce was ready in a salad bowl, along with garden grown tomatoes on a tray and her secret Ritz Bleu Cheese dressing in the food processor.

"Hi honey…it's so great to be home – everything looks just wonderful," said Marlon as he walked up behind her and kissed her neck. She turned and gave him a hug ruffling his hair. "How about a glass of chardonnay?"

"You bet," he said as he reached up in the cabinet and took down two wine glasses. Avis uncorked a bottle of Louis

Jadot Chardonnay Bourgogne and poured. "Here's to us!"

They sat down at the old whaler dining table already set with Burlington-made plates, cutlery, and a basket of warm almond croissants. "When do you expect our son?" asked Marlon.

"Oh, right after practice – another twenty minutes or so." But her smile disappeared and her eyes looked tearful as she said, "Ah, there was a long article in the *Easthampton Star* today about Aldean – it was about the fire." It was hard for her to say it. She knew Marlon was in charge of the fire investigation and the death of Aldean in it.

"It's sure not going to be the same out here now, with him gone!" He liked sharing his cases with Avis; she was a good listener and a calm, reliable adversary in arguing motive.

"Hey, I just heard a car door. It's our Main Man." She was full of joy as she met him at the front door where one of their neighbors had dropped him off.

"Good to see you, son. Go wash up and come join us for supper," called Marlon. He was struck by the fact that his boy would soon be a man. He was growing up fast.

They enjoyed a wonderful supper and had a spirited conversation mostly about his son's school and his sport's routine until Marlon pushed back his chair. "Um, I brought some work home tonight." He looked at both of them. "May I be excused?"

"Oh, of course, dear," said Avis. Soon Gabriel joined in, "You bet, Dad."

Gabriel had known Aldean since he was in grade school and had played on the summer softball team coached by Aldean over the years. Gabe admired him and wanted to become a writer, too. He looked over at his father. "Anything new on the fire, Dad?"

"No, but that's part of my work tonight. We just got the autopsy report and some of the ballistics…." Marlon couldn't finish his sentence. He quickly got up, grabbed his briefcase, and headed up the stairs to his study.

# # #

After closing the study door, he retrieved the thick manila envelope holding the reports and laid them on his desk. He lit a cigarette and stood for a moment looking out the window at the view of Sag Harbor. He savored the view a little longer than usual – he did not look forward to his work this evening.

The autopsy report of Suffolk County was prepared by Chief Medical Examiner Mitchell Marcuse, M.D. for Aldean Reynard Matheson, Age 57 Years and Six Months. As he turned the pages, Detective Samuels realized that he had learned quite a while ago to mentally detach himself from becoming emotionally involved when reading autopsy reports. But he had to admit, that after watching his first autopsy many years ago, he really never got used to it. He had to constantly remind himself of their importance as a trove of evidence into the real truth of why that person had died.

He started to read the findings. "The so-called pugilistic attitude is the result of the shrinkage of muscles and tendons. The internal organs are considerably reduced in size because of fluid loss and consumption by the fire. Heat-related fluid shifts have caused vesicular detachment of the epidermis or false burn blisters, on the skin. There are pseudo-hemorrhages in the form of heat hematomas inside the body. "

He just about lost it when he came to the phrase, "his skull was almost completely intact, leaving the brain in relatively good shape." *That marvelous, brilliant brain, still ready to go, but now denied a body.* He skimmed the identification or composite ID's that indicated that due to the charred condition of the body, DNA was not sufficient by itself to make a match and would have to be supplemented by dental X-rays, body X-rays, fingerprints, photos, a tattoo, and burned objects such as a watch and a ring.

He read that Aldean's long-time assistant and researcher, Stella Levine, had appeared at the Suffolk County morgue, ready to facilitate the findings in the death of her treasured employer; who some said was more than a friend. She was very helpful in providing the ME with Matheson's Porsche, parked lately in her garage, that had his fingerprints all over the steering wheel, his sweat on the seats, his gum stuck on the dash, and empty beer cans littered throughout. She identified the ring as a gift from a long-time girlfriend in California and the watch had been his father's. She provided the name of his prosthodontist in Easthampton for dental records.

Her request to say good-bye to Aldean's corpse was denied due to the horrendous condition it was in. The ME was sincerely concerned that Ms. Levine would have to be hospitalized for shock.

Marlon was coming to the end of the report: The autopsy had been classified as a Class A findings that were inconsistent with the continuation of life. The ME's findings differed from the CSI's done at the death scene as "suffocation by fire being the cause and manner of death" and had concluded, " a male body, charred, ground floor, no noticeable accelerant poured over or near body, brought by ambulance in body bag to Suffolk County morgue in Hauppauge, New York."

Suddenly Samuel's world turned upside down as he continued to read. "Fire victim Matheson suffered a single gunshot wound in the back with bullet entering the left rib cage and angling upward through the right clavicle prior to the fire; the trajectory obtained by means of a long metal probe." As he read the ME's conclusion, shock was setting in. "The body caught fire after death, no soot in mouth. Fire alarm perhaps activated sooner than assailant expected and body excavated by fire crew before being totally cremated."

His hand was shaking as he reached for the ballistics report on the Smith & Wesson model 39-2 manufactured until 1982 and legally purchased by Aldean Matheson in 1985. He was the registered owner of said gun retrieved from the burial site in the yard of Matheson's property on Sunday evening by Detective Samuels of the East Hampton Town Police, aided by W.D. Caldwell, a deputized private investigator with the Handler Agency in Malibu in a chain of custody transaction. Caldwell had been an eye witness to the burial of the evidence and on site just an hour before the fire broke out.

The report was brief and indicated that the bullet found on the gurney, under the charred body of the victim, had been fired from the buried Smith & Wesson pistol. The bullet and the firearm were in good condition. Samuels knew that all guns have unique markings inside the barrel that leave a precise impression on any bullet fired; akin to a fingerprint. He glanced at the rest of the report examining the striations and citing the direction of the bullet as a primary piece of evidence in the homicide. The direction and trajectory help triangulate where the shooter may have been standing and other details such as height etc. In this case it was surmised the shooter was between five feet four inches to five feet six inches and standing behind the victim who was six feet tall.

There was a knock on his study door. But he did not respond.

"Honey, are you in there?" It was Avis and she turned the doorknob quietly while pushing in a cart with Marlon's favorite shell-shaped cookies and a big pot of cocoa. Marlon stared at her like he'd just seen a ghost.

"Oh, Marlon, what's wrong?" She'd only seen this shocked expression one other time – when they'd pulled his father's lifeless body out of a car accident near Wainscott. She steeled herself for a tragic revelation.

"He was shot, Avis. He died before the fire started…or set. Avis, it was a homicide."

"What!" Avis felt like she was going to faint and fell onto the sofa. She lay like that for a few minutes, but Marlon seemed not to notice. Suddenly she rolled over and started screaming – a series of staccato keening gurgles. Then she began to weep, tears running down unabated. "No, No! It can't be. Who would do such a thing? Why would anyone kill Aldean?"

Suddenly the door flew open, banging the wall, as Gabe rushed in. "Mom, Dad! What's wrong?"

"Oh, son, he was murdered," cried Avis. "Our Aldean was murdered!" In an instant, both Marlon and Avis seemed to be aware of the terrible impact this news had on their son, the one whom they both loved so much. They stood up together and reached out to him, to hold him, and comfort him.

28

Wednesday afternoon W.D. made the transfer from LaGuardia airport for the flight to LAX and started to relax. He had placed Prince in a dog kennel after his papers and ticket were approved. He'd decided to have the dog slightly sedated for the long flight. W.D. felt like he was on a high wire series of events and he was exhilarated by it.

Renee stood off to the side waving at W.D. from the luggage area of the L.A. airport. Like two magnets, they headed for each other. "Oh, hon, it's so good to see you again." They hugged and W.D. felt like it had been years since he'd seen his wife. After settling Prince down they had a taxi drive them to a Travel Lodge motel where W.D. had reserved a suite.

During a dinner of crab cakes, broccoli salad, and white wine, at a nearby café, Renee caught him up on time spent at the Mulholland Drive home of Dyanna Dahlberg. She had been invited to stay there and visit with Gunhilde and Anita. They discussed everything except W.D.'s recent expedition.

After dinner, Renee and W.D. returned to the suite. He planned to read the Xeroxed copies of the material buried in Montauk and the papers found in Joyce's cabin. While

W.D. settled into a recliner with a sleepy Prince by his side; Renee went to bed, happy that her mate was with her.

W.D. carefully opened the briefcase. First off, he read the copy of the will that had been in the cabin. He was totally surprised to read that Aldean had left his entire estate including the copyrights of his books to Joyce Santa Anna nee Jyaana Shakti Densmore of Oxnard, California. The name Densmore bothered him. He'd heard it before. He thought about the Smith & Wesson they'd found in the metal box. He checked his photo of the gun. He wondered what, if anything, the detectives had found out about the owner of it.

Who was Joyce Santa Anna? Didn't she work for Swinburne's oil company? What was she doing with Aldean Matheson? Why did she have a one-way ticket to Paris in her briefcase?

#   #   #

After he saw Renee and Prince off Thursday morning, W.D. waited for David in front of the motel. Soon the Jeep pulled up and David called out, "Hey, W.D. good to see you. Jump in." He put his luggage in the back, "Chris is waiting anxiously for you."

"Yeah, it's good to be back."

W.D. settled into the Jeep. He noticed that Handler had thoughtfully arranged some juices and bottled water for him. They rode along in silence until they arrived at the entrance to Chris's' home and office.

Chris met him at the door,"Hey, W.D. great job. I am so impressed." Chris steered W.D. over to the patio and seating area. He had coffee and scones set out on the small side table.

"Yes, well, I really enjoyed the job," said W.D. "I frankly

didn't know if I had it in me – especially the creepy crawl business."

"Well, you have it in you and you made a big dent in the case. We are finding that your surveillance has opened up some other threads of criminality – which I will explain in a moment." Chris poured them both coffee.

"Let me start right out by saying we have made a connection between Aldean Matheson and R. Proctor Swinburne." Chris started to smile and then said, "They have Joyce Santa Anna in common."

"Oh, is that right?" W.D. was surprised, "they do?"

"We had the posse in Oxnard working on who she was, especially since she was traveling with Matheson that Friday night from LAX to LaGuardia International Airport." He leaned back and then continued, "They found out that although she was cited as part of the Environ-Oil secretarial pool, she was really an assistant to R. Proctor Swinburne, son of the late owner." Chris stopped momentarily, "it seems her real name is Densmore."

Chris consulted some papers and re-arranged them so he could follow the narrative and yet still speak off the cuff:

"It appears that in the 1970's, Aldean Matheson was a visiting professor in English at the University of California, Berkeley. He fell in love with one of his students, Jyaana Densmore. She moved in with him after dropping out of college. They lived on a street called Bonita for over a year and it became a serious relationship. Aldean wanted to get married." Chris stopped as he considered this. "But instead of getting hitched, Jyaana got a job at a radio station as an intern and later as a disc jockey using the moniker Joyce Santa Anna."

W.D. was astonished. "My God, I guess we'd better follow

up on that."

"Oh, we already have," said Chris. "Get another coffee and sit down. We have more revelations, my man." Chris sat back and put his feet up on the low table.

"It was while Joyce was working at a big radio station in San Francisco that she met Wade Tarintina, the local newscaster and radio personality."

"What? Wade worked there?"

"Yeah, and I guess Joyce took a fancy to Wade and they started an affair while she was still living with Aldean." Chris sat back and looked at his notes and then continued, "Wade was married at the time to a really crazy woman and she decided to sue Joyce for alienation of affection culminating in her making death threats after Wade was hired at the top Los Angeles radio station and became very popular."

"Wowie. That's right out of the tabloids. Who would have guessed?" W.D. shook his head in disbelief.

Chris looked out of the window and reflected a bit. "Well, it ended badly. Mrs. Tarintina shot Joyce, and seriously wounded her. The wife won the lawsuit, but Joyce was hospitalized and ultimately fired from her job while Wade Tarintina went on to more fame and fortune."

"Did they arrest Mrs. Tarintina?"

"No, Joyce agreed to drop the charges if she gave Wade a divorce."

"Huh. What happened to Joyce?"

"She had a godfather named R. Proctor Swinburne who took care of everything – paid the bills, the legal fees, and topped it off with a job at Environ-Oil."

Chris was coming to the end of his narrative.

"This was all too much for Aldean. He resigned his

professorship and returned to Long Island. But not without threatening to kill Wade for taking Joyce from him."

W.D. frowned; and sat for awhile, mulling over the information. "Was Swinburne in love with her, too?"

"Oh probably, but he was already married."

"How does any of this explain Swinburne's desperate attempts to buy my land?" W.D. bit into a scone, enjoying it immensely.

"Chris thought a bit and then said, "He might have wanted to become a bigger tycoon than his father."

"Hmmm. How does one go about nailing all this weird stuff down and what does one do with it?" W.D. looked puzzled.

"You are exactly right. It doesn't do much except make excuses." Chris looked away. "You know, we have to continue our investigation of Santa Anna. She's the key here. Why Tarintina was assaulted and left for dead and why Aldean really did end up dead."

W.D. looked over at Chris in amusement. "Is this Stage Two, son?"

"Yeah, it is. I'd like a recon of Environ-Oil and what Joyce did there. And you are just the man, W.D."

"Huh? Hey, no more creepy crawls. I am retired. Do you hear me?"

"Oh, no more of that. What would you say to a drive down to Oxnard and a visit to the Environ-Oil under the guise of a CBS Production staffer checking locations?"

"Ahhhhh, sure. How do I do that?"

"I've had Walberg clear the way for a call from CBS made to Environ-Oil requesting some interior shots of their company for a documentary. Then I had a limited number of CBS business cards made up for you to use while there. The telephone number on the card is Wheelock and they will answer the line confirming who you are, but will only take a message."

"Sounds good to me," W.D. started to get excited, "Yeah, think I'll wear my panama straw hat."

Chris stood up and reached over to pick up a wrapped box on a coffee table.

"W.D. I have a gift for you. This is to show my appreciation for the great job done in the Hamptons." He passed it over to him.

"Well that's thoughtful of you, son."

He unwrapped the package and opened up the box revealing a Rolex watch.

"Uh, my goodness, I can't accept this." W.D. was surprised by the luxury item.

"I insist," said Chris. "It's a replica of a 1954 Rolex designed for Sir Edmund Hilary, the first man to reach the summit of Mount Everest."

"Thank you, son." W.D. put the watch on his left wrist and then said, "Golly, it feels good."

W.D. admired his new watch and thought he'd now have to read up on Sir Hilary. "I sure do like this watch and I'm honored to wear it."

Then they got down to details such as the Friday morning departure to Oxnard by W.D. and David, and how the Jeep was fitted out as an office. Chris outlined the stops on the way, the possible scenarios at the Environ-Oil guardhouse, and what to do if there was trouble.

Chris settled W.D. into the guest room and they said good night. W.D. slept like a log.

29

After one stop they arrived at Environ-Oil a little after nine. W.D. was amazed to find that the business complex was a gated property. He was not expecting anything like this. David pulled into the driveway and was met by a guard. W.D. said he was there to meet a Mr. Benjamin Swinburne, CEO who had given permission to make a list of prospective interior shots for a CBS documentary. Chris had assured W.D. that Santa Anna was still in a cell in Easthampton awaiting someone to pay her bail. He handed over his CBS business card and waited while the guard made a telephone call.

"Yes, sir, please proceed to the front of the building and someone will meet you in the lobby and show you around." The guard waved them through.

"I'll park in the Visitor's Parking," said David. "I'll wait there for you."

W.D. got out of the Jeep and headed over to the lobby. The grounds were beautifully landscaped and a small pool with a fountain burbled nearby. He was met at the door by a woman with red hair, in her late fifties, an obvious scar across her forehead.

"Greetings, Mr. Caldwell, my name is Sirina; and I am Mr. Ben Swinburne's secretary."

"Wonderful to meet you," said W.D., "we are pleased to be able to have permission to use footage from your facility in our program."

"Oh, glad to oblige. Would you like a coffee?" She half-turned before he answered. "I will send in Mr. Swinburne's secretary to help you."

" Thank you, I would appreciate her assistance and the coffee."

She retreated, leaving W.D. to his own devices. He looked at the oil paintings and was very impressed by one of a large strawberry field painted and signed by a well known artist. After about ten minutes Sirina had not returned. W.D cautiously looked into an open door off to the right. It appeared to be a conference room and was very elegant. W.D. decided to step in and look around at the various prints all framed and lit with a small art light. He wondered what was keeping Sirina as more than fifteen minutes had passed since she left for the coffee.

As he turned to look at the back wall he was surprised to see a large map of the US Pipeline System. He moved closer, then stepped right up to the map, and stared at it with a puzzled look. *Why that's the area around the Clearbrook Tank Terminal.* His eyes roamed west of Clearbrook and he saw the small towns of Gonvick, Gully, and Trail. He noticed that Trail was circled in red. He was shocked to see that the area included his property purchased from Steve Olsen and presently up for sale.

"My God, what's this?" he mumbled out loud. He didn't know what a big deal buying his land was.

He was so involved that he did not hear someone enter the room until he heard the swish of fabric and realized someone was standing right behind him. He heard a familiar voice: "What are you doing in here, you snoopy old bastard?" He then felt a gun muzzle in his back. "Stay where you are and put your hands up on the wall."

W.D. complied quickly.

"Ah, there must be some mistake; I'm only here to search locations for CBS." W.D. was alarmed that he'd been caught unawares without his weapon.

"I'm going to take care of you now, so you'll never be a problem again unless you sign this."

There was a rustling of papers and the gun was removed from his back. He turned and looked right into the hard face of Joyce Santa Anna.

"Surprised to see me, are you?"

"Well, ah, no ma'am, not really. Have we met before?"

"Don't play coy with me, you old coot." She looked at him with pure hatred. "Get your ass over here and sign this."

W.D. picked up the pen on the table and pretended to read the document. But he'd read it before and knew its content. It was another purchase agreement on his property in Trail.

"Get this signed right now." She hissed. "Then we're going for a ride."

W.D. thought of the huge life insurance policy that Chris had on him. God, he was glad that Renee would be taken care of. He felt faint and weak in his legs, while trembling noticeably.

He started to sign the document, the gun pressed into his neck. Suddenly he heard a man's voice from the doorway.

"You aren't going anywhere! Drop your weapon and put your hands up. NOW!"

It was David and he had a Glock 9mm semi-automatic pistol trained on Joyce. She turned quickly as if to fire at him, but W.D. adeptly stepped forward and grabbed the gun muzzle with his left hand pushing upward while twisting it out of her hands with the right. David kept his gun trained on her, and told her to put her hands up. He nodded at W.D. who then stepped forward and picked up the weapon to empty it of the bullets. He was utterly shocked to see an orange cap on the tip of the muzzle. My God, it was only a replica! He put it back on the table with shaking hands.

Joyce started to swear in what W.D. thought was a most shocking manner. He'd never heard some of those curse words before. "The police will be here shortly," she said, "I pressed the switch under the table and they'll arrest both of you stupid assholes." She started spitting at David.

Two burly policemen immediately appeared in the doorway, handcuffs clearly visible. "Hold it right there. Oxnard Police."

"You sure got here fast! Arrest these two jerks for trespassing and attempted robbery," said Joyce. She glared at W.D and David. "Right now."

The younger cop moved toward Joyce and told her to put her hands out so he could cuff her. "No, not me you dumbfuck!" She began screaming at the two cops and ran for the door. The second cop tackled her and she scratched his face with her long nails. She spit on him and pulled his hair. They fell to the floor and rolled over and over; Joyce kicking and biting him. One of the policemen looked over at David and said, "Thanks for the tip! Please call or stop by the station and give us your statement."

After being somewhat subdued by brute force, she sobbed out a disconnected ramble of words.

"You better come with us, ma'am," said the first cop. "You can tell us all about it downtown." The second cop reached across the table, picked up her fake gun with a small tissue, and slipped it into a large evidence bag.

W.D. started to shake all over after the gun was removed. What if it had been real? He quickly reached into his pocket for medication for high-blood pressure. He took it without water and prayed he wouldn't have a stroke. "I'm just too damned old now to be out here on this kind of business, David," he said as he started to fall backwards.

David recognized W.D.'s dilemma. "Hey, man, let me help you out to the Jeep. Ah, I have some Starbucks coffee out there in a thermos with a little whiskey in it."

"My God, David, you saved my life showing up with that gun. I was never so happy to see anybody. Ever!"

"Yeah, always on the alert. That's me. I was the bodyguard for Herschel and now, of course, for Chris."

"Oh, my – that's interesting! Thank you so much…oh, so much." W.D. grabbed the contract for deed, partially signed by him, and he limped out to the Jeep, holding onto David's arm. After getting into the backseat, taking a big swig of laced coffee, W.D. looked around in relief; he didn't see anyone at all. He supposed the employees were too frightened to appear after the police visit and all that screaming.

They left Environ-Oil and David turned left onto the highway. W.D. glimpsed the swerving police car up ahead and a female with long black hair swishing it from side to side in the back seat, as if in a frenzy of rage. He knew who it was, and for once he felt sorry for the cops.

30

East Hampton Police Chief Edwin Norquist wrapped up the meeting that stunned the police department: Aldean Matheson had been murdered. After the ME announced the results of the autopsy and the ballistic report there were a lot of questions. Now a famous author, rich and widely admired, had been killed in his home, shot in the back and set on fire. Who had committed this horrendous crime? Why?

They had a big investigation on their hands. While the chief was busy with their public relations officer in sending out a press release; Detective Marlon Samuels was busy trying to round up witnesses, both family and friends who could help him find out who did this. A press conference was set up for Monday morning in Wainscott to announce the murder investigation.

Back in his office, Samuels knew he had to work fast. He was in charge of documenting social history of the deceased – marital, family, sexual, employment and financial. He wanted to do interviews with key people before the murder was announced. He tried to make up a list of people to interview, but he needed help. He turned to his secretary, "Linda, please get Stella Levine on the phone and ask her to come in for an interview today." Samuels knew she had worked for Matheson for years and would be a good place to start. She agreed to come into his office at 3:00 p.m.

Stella arrived right on the dot. Samuels was surprised by her androgynous appearance. She was a woman in her late fifties, short and stout, a big bosom, dressed in a tailored suit with a man's tie. She had beautiful fingernails and obviously had frequent manicures. She wore what looked like a graduation ring and an expensive looking watch with diamonds in the band. Her only makeup was a light rose lipstick.

"Ms. Levine, thank you for coming in." Samuels took her hand and held it. "Please come over here and sit down. I have a few questions for you." He pointed to a table with two chairs. "I hope we can get some answers that will help us clear up the reason for the fire and the tragic death of Aldean Matheson."

"Yes, Detective Samuels, I am glad to cooperate. You know I loved that man, more than anyone will ever know and I-I ...I can't adjust myself to his being gone...forever."

"Yes, it's hard to believe he's dead. You have my sincere sympathy."

She took a chair opposite Samuels and plunked her purse down on the floor.

"Would you like a cigarette, Stella?"

"Yes, sir. I would." He handed her an ashtray and she reached down and took out a pack of Marlboro's and a lighter from her purse. She inhaled deeply and he could see her body relax.

"Stella, I know you worked for Mr. Matheson – Aldean – for about twenty-five years. You were a trusted associate. You came forth and supplied the ME with very helpful information. Now we need to know what was going on in his private life before his death. Who are his friends? Does he have a family we can interview? Also was he working on a book now? Did he have anyone who might wish him harm, any arguments?"

She thought for awhile. "It's hard to narrate his recent life. He always had a very complex lifestyle. He was impulsive, but extremely regimented. He had friends, some for many, many years. But he had no family. He called himself an orphan and it was literally true."

"I hope you can give us a few names, addresses and or telephone numbers?"

"Of course," she said and reached down into her purse and pulled out a sheet of paper. "Here are a few names of friends and professionals contacts that I prepared after you called."

"Were you working for Aldean at the present time?"

"Yes."

"When did you see him last?

"I worked for him all day Saturday – the day before the fire. He was working on a sequel to his book about oil tycoons. I typed up some interviews he'd done. He'd only been back a week, arriving in Montauk the previous Friday night from Los Angeles."

"Did he travel alone from LAX ?"

"Ah, no. He brought an old friend with him – actually an ex-girlfriend named Joyce Santa Anna."

"I see. Did she stay with him for the week leading up to the fire?"

"Yes, I believe she did."

"Did they get along? Were there any arguments between them?"

"Ahhh no. They weren't getting along. It seemed that Joyce had become quite angry with him and had threatened to leave and…." She stopped and started shaking, her face quivered, and then the tears came. She got up, grabbed her purse, and left the room.

Samuels knew talking about Aldean was too much for her. Grief caught up with her. He'd get back in touch with her later. She was a good woman. She'd stepped up and done what a family member would have for Aldean.

He picked up the single sheet of paper with neat typing. It only had three names on it: a neighbor, a girlfriend, and his publisher; all with their address, telephone number and relationship to the victim.

He decided to get started and called the neighbor Don Oatley of Montauk. He lived next to Aldean and was recently retired. He dialed the number.

"Hullo."

"Good evening. Is this Mr. Oatley?

"Who's interested?"

"Mr. Oatley, this is Detective Marlon Samuels with the East Hampton Police. We'd like to ask you a few questions about your neighbor, Aldean Matheson. Can you come into the station in Wainscott?"

"Huh! I've been waitin' fer you to call. Can't you come out here and see me? I ain't got the gas money to be runnin' around especially if it's for that old woman-chaser Aldean."

"Well, Mr. Oatley, we could ask a few questions over the telephone. It would be tape recorded. I could call you in the morning. If we needed to follow up on anything, then we'll make a trip out to your home."

"Yeah, yeah. Okay. Lived next to him for 20 years. Tape recorded? Yeah, that's okay. I'm busy now. I'm feeding the animals – got rabbits, two skunks, a yellow lab, and ten chickens." He hung up.

Next Marlon called Lynette Larson. The telephone rang four times and then a recorded voice answered. "This is Lynette and Aldean, Junior. Please leave us a message, we'll call back." There was a sound effect of a baby gurgling. This surprised Samuels. What the hell. A baby? He left a message and asked that she reply as soon as possible. He left his home number as well.

Then he called Matthew Franken, Aldean's publisher with a New York City address. Mr. Franken also had a recorded message on his line. It was crisp and to the point." This is Matthew Franken. Please leave me a brief message with time and date. Thank you for calling." Again Marlon left a message and gave both his police and his home number to call. The phone rang immediately after he'd hung up and a female voice said, "This is Mr. Franken's secretary. He has left for the day, but I will make sure he calls you this evening. He has been expecting a call from you and will cooperate fully in this tragic incident."

Incident? Marlon was stupefied by that reference. No, I think not. Murder, fire, destroying a home, a life, and a fabulous career. Well, this will be an interesting interview. In fact, he thought all three of them would be.

31

After they returned to Malibu, David left W.D. off in front of the residence and pulled the Jeep into one of the three garages.

"Hey, W.D. Another great job. Thanks! Hey, come on up and take a seat – got some new developments," Chris was standing on the stair step waving at him.

"What's up?" Although he'd already filled Chris in on the Oxnard trip via the Fax in the Jeep office, he wondered if the Oxnard police had more news.

"Uh, the Oxnard Police have a confession from Joyce Santa Anna. She broke down in the interview room."

"Well, well. Yeah, I thought she looked like she was crackin' up."

"The gist of it is that she admitted she was an overnight guest of Aldean's home before it caught fire."

"Oh, really. My God, that's something."

"Joyce claimed she was upstairs asleep while Mr. Matheson watched television downstairs with her dog, Prince."

"Oh, yeah?"

"She said she was awakened by smoke detectors and ran downstairs to find Matheson struggling to put out the flames from a cigarette that had swept through his pajamas.

She threw a blanket and a rug on him, but couldn't put out the fire."

"Huh!"

"She said the house then filled with thick, black smoke and after sustaining burns, she grabbed the dog and fled the house. She got into her Jeep and headed over to the Montauk Highway. She claimed she couldn't see much because of the smoke, and then she heard the house explode." Handler laid the paper down. "It seems that when she arrived at Gurney's Inn, that she'd already rented a cabin for herself and the dog, and she did not report the fire or her participation in it."

"Why not?" W. D. was upset by this. "She might have saved his life?"

"After you made the citizen's arrest, she was held by East Hampton Police but they did not have enough evidence to hold her. Bail was paid by R. Proctor Swinburne and she returned to California."

Chris continued: "She's being held overnight at the Oxnard Police City Jail and then, perhaps, back to the East Hampton Police jurisdiction as a witness to the deadly fire that claimed the life of Matheson that's still under investigation."

Just then they heard the clicking of the FAX machine as a long Fax made its way into the office of Chris Handler revealing details of the autopsy, and news of the bullet that killed Aldean Matheson before the fire consumed him. Also a shocking new will, signed, and on file at the Town Clerk's Office in the East Hampton Court House.

32

It was a quiet Saturday morning at the East Hampton Police Station. Detective Samuels was still using Stella's list of Aldean's neighbor, girlfriend, and publisher; he planned to question them closely and tape record them. He did not want to tip his hand by requesting they come to the station which would have put them on the alert. He knew Monday's upcoming press conference announcing the homicide would make all the difference in the perception of the case and change how friends or family responded to questioning.

At 9:00 a.m. he called Don Oatley who answered on the first ring. "Good morning, Don, this is Detective Samuels and I'd like to interview you. I need your permission to tape record our conversation."

"Sure thing, Officer. Go ahead and record me. I'm at your service." Samuels then ID'd the tape and proceeded:

"Mr. Oatley, how long have you lived next to Aldean Matheson?"

"Oh, around twenty years…give or take a few months."

"Did you have a good relationship with Mr. Matheson?"

"Ah, no."

"Why?"

"Well, he always had so much company – made too much

noise – he was an old windbag."

"Did he have a lot of company the week preceding the fire?"

"Yes. He had a lot of deliveries. He also had a lot of pickups by FedEx. He was repairing some parts of his house and had several construction workers there – hammering away."

"Did you see Aldean on Saturday or Saturday night before the fire?"

"Oh. Yes, I did. He was wearing a pair of shorts and a tee shirt. He seemed to be limping because he was using a cane."

"Was he alone?"

"No, Stella had been there all day and she worked up to around nine in the evening and ah – when she left she took Aldean's car. I thought that was kind of odd. He also had that little bitch there mouthin' off with that nasty little dog – barkin' all the time."

"Who was that – with the dog?"

"Oh, some woman from California."

"How late were you up Saturday night – when was the last time you saw Matheson's house intact?"

"Hmmm. Around eleven or so I went to bed. I know I looked out the window before I lay down and saw lights on in his house."

"When did you smell smoke? When do you think the fire started?"

"Oh, huh? Maybe four or so in the mornin'. I know I smelled smoke about that time cuz I thought it was my place that was on fire. But when I looked out the window I saw smoke billowing from his house and I called 911 right away."

"Is there anything you want to tell me about Aldean and the fire?"

"No, not really. I think it was arson, you know. Aldean was a womanizer and I think this backfired on him somehow."

"Thank you, Mr. Oatley. That's it for now. If we need more info we will visit you in Montauk or bring you into the station."

"Okay, Officer. Glad to help."

This was certainly a careful interview on the part of Oatley. Yet, he knew that Oatley had been a bombastic neighbor after checking his criminal record. He'd had five DUI's in the past ten years and a car accident three years ago. He'd been cited for trespassing on Matheson's property and making terroristic threats. Oatley filed a civil suit against Aldean two years ago for damaging trees on his property. The case was dismissed because it was determined that the property and the trees belonged to Aldean. Actually Oatley had done a great job of dodging his questions. Now it was time to move on to the next interview. It had to be Franken, his publisher. He just couldn't deal with a woman and a baby right now. He decided to take a quick break and went down a flight of stairs to the reception room where the watch commander Archie was answering the telephone.

"Hey, Archie, any coffee?"

"Nah, not any good coffee. I was just about to ask if you'd brought the thermos?"

"Oh, yes, I did. It's out in the car. Just a minute." His wife always filled a double thermos for him and he was so grateful for it this morning. He came back in and poured a cup for Archie and then went back up to his office and poured himself a cup before calling New York.

"Good morning. May I speak to Mr. Franken, please?"

"Oh, good morning – Inspector Samuels, is it?"

"Yes, it is. I'd like to ask you a few questions regarding

Aldean Matheson. I'd like your permission to tape record our conversation."

"Ah, of course, you can record our chat. I hope I can be of help."

Detective Samuels ID'd the tape and proceeded:

"How long have you known Aldean Matheson, Mr. Franken?"

"Hmmm. It's about twenty years now. We've been his publisher for all his best sellers."

"Did his books sell well? Are you his only publisher?"

"Goodness, yes, his books made a fortune. We are his exclusive publisher. Initially he was with a rival publisher, but we lured him away."

"I see. Did you have a good relationship?"

"No, I can't say we did, actually."

"Why not?"

"Aldean never got his books in on time and we lost a lot of money due to missing our sales deadlines."

"When is the last time you saw Aldean?"

"Oh, about a month ago. He was in New York to see his lawyer—something about changing his will—and he stopped in for coffee."

"Did the lawyer's visit concern your relationship?"

"No, I guess it had something to do with one of his women."

"Was Aldean working on a new book?"

"No…ah…but he was working on a prime time TV special."

"Do you know his friends or family?"

"Well, he doesn't have a family. He's an orphan. I met Stella, his secretary and Lynette, his girl friend. I don't know any other friends, to speak of."

"Did he have any enemies? Anyone that wished him harm?"

"Yes, he did. There was a TV producer in Los Angeles who hated him. He'd also recently had several death threats – right after he published the book about the L.A. oilfields."

"Were the threats reported to the police?"

"Yes, I believe they were reported to the LAPD about two months ago."

"Is there anything else you'd like to tell me about Aldean or the fire?"

"No.

"Thank you, Mr. Franken, for your time. If we need more detail, we will be back in touch."

"Okay, Inspector. Sounds good. Have a nice evening."

Samuels sat back in his chair and reflected. Obviously Franken was a whiner and was probably hard to work for. He'd looked up his criminal record, but found nothing except that a former female employee had charged him with sexual assault about five years ago. But the case was dismissed due to lack of evidence.

He put the cover back on his thermos, straightened up some papers on his desk, and decided to head for home.

33

"Oh, my dear Marlon, I'm so glad to see you," said Avis, "there's been several calls from a woman who says she needs to talk to you about Aldean. It's urgent."

Samuels took her hand and held it. "I hope I haven't upset you. I left my home number for witnesses to call – I presume it was Lynette Larson?"

"Hmm, no, it was Janine Larson, the sister of Lynette, and she'd like to talk to you as soon as possible."

Samuels had a station tape recorder up in his study and decided to call her from there. "When is dinner being served, sweetheart? I could make this call now and get it off my mind."

"No problem, we'll dine at 7:00 p.m. an hour from now. So please, take care of business. Anyway Gabe won't be home before seven anyway."

He entered his study and set up the tape recorder. He'd had questions prepared for Lynette but now realized they'd have to be changed in light of it being a relative. He dialed the number in East Hampton and it was answered promptly.

"This is Janine Larson, may I help you?"

"Yes, Janine, this is Detective Marlon Samuels with the East Hampton Police. I need to ask you some questions regarding our investigation of the fire and loss of Aldean Matheson's life. I need your permission to tape record this conversation."

"I am so glad you called, Detective. Yes, you can tape record. You have my permission. In fact, I prefer this to coming into the station."

"Janine, I understand you are Lynette Larson's sister? Is she available for an interview now?"

"Well, no, she's not. Lynette is in the Southampton Hospital with what is commonly called a nervous breakdown. She was in the ICU for the last week under sedation. Yesterday they moved her to a private room. She wants to talk to the police. She wants you to visit her in her room as she has much to tell you."

"Yes, I will certainly do that. Would Sunday – tomorrow morning – say, at 9:00 a.m. be a good time?"

"Yes, that would be the best possible time. This evening is not good because she has been tranquilized and is sleeping soundly."

"Janine, I just have one question for you. The others can wait for Lynette. I hope you will join us tomorrow morning?"

"Yes, I will be there. Go ahead and ask me the question. I'll do my best to answer it."

"Did Lynette have a baby with Aldean?"

"Yes, she did. He was born about six months ago. She had a little boy. Aldean was shocked by the pregnancy and demanded proof of paternity. He had the latest DNA test that I believe concluded probability of paternity at 99.9 %. He realized it was his baby and was very excited about having a son. Their relationship changed overnight."

"Let's leave it there, Janine. I appreciate your call and I look forward to meeting both of you tomorrow."

"Yes, same here. Good night, Detective." They both hung up.

Samuels sat back and reflected. This was not what he expected to hear about Lynette's mental health. He felt sadness for her predicament. He recalled that a deep state of shock can make it difficult to get reliable information from a witness. He shut the lights off and turned to leave his study, anxious to join his wife and son. He was glad to leave the sorrow of this case and enjoy the happiness of being with his family.

34

Detective Samuels entered Southampton Hospital surprised to see a security guard ready to check his ID. He said he was a detective and there to interview Lynette Larson on police business. He showed his badge and was told to take a private elevator up to the fourth floor where a nurse would meet him and take him to Ms. Larson's room.

"Good morning officer, please follow me," said the nurse as she walked a short ways down the hall and then turned into a room.

Samuels saw two blonde women: one sitting in a chair wearing a white gown tied at the waist; the other standing up behind her in a long, white tee shirt, carefully brushing her long silken hair. He was struck by how much they looked like a fourth century statue of two young Greek females – athletic and big boned with placid expressions.

"Good morning, Detective Samuels, this is my sister Lynette and she is eager to talk with you." Janine put the brush down and found a chair for Samuels.

"Good morning, Janine and Lynette." He stepped over to take Lynette's hand and held it in sympathy. He bent close to her and said "Lynette, I want to ask you a few questions and I need your permission to tape record it?"

She looked up at him, her eyes brimming with tears, trying to hold herself together, "I give you my permission, Detective, and I have so much to get off my mind. It's bothering me terribly. My life is over, ruined forever, without Aldean!"

Samuels thought she was going to start crying. But she surprised him. She started talking instead, seemingly impelled by a sudden rage underlying her grief.

Samuels quickly ID'd the tape as she continued to talk nonstop: "After I had the baby, Aldean fell in love with me. He'd had a DNA test and paternity was confirmed. Shortly after that, he proposed to me. We filed our marriage license about a month ago and the wedding was to be held a week from today in Amagansett." She caught her breath. "Aldean had a huge problem with an evil woman who'd latched onto him years ago. She was like cancer. Her name is Joyce Santa Anna. She'd called me when she was staying with Aldean and said she was going to kill me and the baby. After her threat, Janine hired a security firm 24 hours a day to watch over me."

Lynette stopped talking, her breathing rapid, and a slight drool running down the side of her mouth. Detective Samuels glanced at Janine, who was disturbed by the painful narration from Lynette.

She wiped Lynette's face who then continued: "Aldean changed his will to leave everything to me and the baby. I know Joyce had been in his will, but he removed her entirely. She found out about it and went berserk. She hated me, she hated the baby, and then she hated Aldean. I know she shot him in cold blood and I know she set fire to Aldean's home, our home – it was arson. I want you to look into this! Please, please – because Aldean was murdered!" Almost immediately, Lynette fell over on her side, she seemed about to faint.

Janine rang for the nurse who took a look and went to find the doctor. Samuels could see that Lynette was unconscious. He clicked off the tape recorder; he noted that it had been on for fifteen minutes. He hurriedly slipped out of the room as the medical team began resuscitation. Janine saw Samuels leave and ran after him.

"This is not your fault – Detective Samuels – Lynette has been living with this tragedy and she needed to tell you about it. I can verify all that she said for the record. Oh, my God. Pray for her!"

"Yes, I will, Janine. I am so sorry for Lynette. I can promise you that we will seek justice and the guilty will be punished. Lynette has made a strong case for an arrest. Please call me at the station or at home and let me know how she's faring."

He left the hospital and got into the police car. He immediately called Chief Norquist on the car radio about his interview with Lynette Larson. They arranged to meet at the station in an hour to listen to the recording.

Samuels parked in front of the station and sat in the car for a few minutes before going in. He knew Lynette was telling the truth. Now they had to fit the last piece of the puzzle together. Where was Joyce Santa Anna now? He needed to get in touch with W.D. Caldwell right away.

35

Max made a right turn onto Topanga Canyon Boulevard heading to Glendale to pick up an employee of the Pullman Committee who'd been interviewed on a local radio station. Sheldon was slumped down in the passenger seat staring out at the cavalcade of cars, end to end, as far as he could see. They were at work for the Boss, R. Proctor Swinburne.

The elderly gangsters had spent Thursday night *kibitzing* and playing poker with two of their neighbors. "I just don't understand why the Boss gave you this new car." Sheldon glanced at Max and wrinkled his forehead. They were traveling in the latest model Lincoln Town Car and it was fully loaded.

"Huh? What makes you say that," Max kept his eye on the road.

"Well, we obviously screwed up our last three assignments big time. I will summarize in order of occurrence – I ended up assaulting Vern Mattel instead of killing him. We botched the kidnapping of Caldwell's grandson/employee, and instead of rubbing out Tarintina, you only ran over his arm. You old *schlemiel*."

"FEH! That wasn't my fault. If I'd been driving this car, a Lincoln, that stoolie would have been pulverized."

Sheldon looked aghast. "You'd contemplate using your private car to rub someone out?"

"Nah. But I have to make it clear that the car, in this case, a Saab 9000, is a heavy car and the front wheel drive was off-kilter. It made a big difference in my skill set."

"Listen, you old buzzard, that's just an excuse. Now it's time you shared with me what you know about the Boss!"

"Yeah, yeah, but first you have to understand him…he likes to live on the edge," Max grinned as he looked over at Sheldon. "He empathizes with us."

"What? What are you saying? Is he some kind of a wacko?" Sheldon thought for a moment. "It's time you told me some more about R. Proctor Swinburne, real factual information, not some blurbs." Sheldon sat up straight in the seat ready for Max's report.

"Okay. Fair enough," said Max. "Let's start at the beginning. I'm his uncle, you know, *mishpocheh*."

Sheldon stared at Max totally surprised. He spent a few minutes processing this information and then said, "Well, that explains a lot. Go on."

"I'm going to tell you about his early life – it will explain so much," said Max. He pulled a cigar out of his pocket and lit it at one of their traffic stops. "Proctor liked to fight as a child. He had a buddy who lived next door named Ulysses Densmore, and he did, too."

Max decided to pull over and stopped in a rest area. He then continued after a pause. "It got so bad, the fighting, the scuffling, and animosity of these two friends that Old Man Swinburne, with the approval of Ulysses' parents, went out and bought two pairs of boxing gloves. He gave each of them a pair, then shoved the two scrapping boys into his Ford Woody, and drove them out to the strawberry fields."

"Why'd he do that?" Sheldon was puzzled.

"He stopped the car near a plowed field, put the gloves on the boys, and told them to go at it." Max started to laugh as he recalled the event.

"I don't think that's funny," said Sheldon. "What are you, a sadist?"

"Yeah, maybe I am." Max continued to recount his memory of the fights.

"The boys fought so hard some nights that one of them was usually left nearly unconscious when Senior picked them up off the ground. He used to lay them in the back of the station wagon and they bled all over the upholstery."

"My God, I'm getting sick," said Sheldon. "What the hell was the matter with that old *shmendrik?* He could've killed one of those idiot kids."

"Yeah, I guess so." Max blew out some smoke, his eyes twinkling with what he had to say next.

"Well, five or six of those matches finally ended the fighting. The boys met up with the Old Man and told him they had decided between them to never disagree or ever fight again."

"Huh?"

"They became best friends, went to the same college–Pepperdine University–stood up for each other's weddings, and then went into business together."

"That's one of the weirdest stories I've ever heard," said Sheldon shaking his head in disbelief.

"Uh huh, yet it ended very badly, said Max. "Proctor was accused of manslaughter for trying to kill Ulysses," he paused, "there was an indictment against him."

"My God!"

"Oh. The case was dismissed," said Max calmly. "Old Man Swinburne, his father, got him off. Insanity!"

"Really? He tried to kill his best friend!" Sheldon slid down in the car seat again.

"Well, that's not the worst; he put out a hit on his first wife and almost succeeded. Sammy got him off by citing the Boss's poor eyesight – you know detached retina, the drops caused his eyelashes to grow, blah, blah."

A horrible realization overcame Sheldon. He saw the writing on the wall. So many questions were answered in a way that immobilized him with a sense of suffocating captivity, like being back in jail – never able to leave.

"No wonder he bought you this car! Who else but a relative would work for someone like him – someone with low-moral turpitude." He spit it out angrily, enraged by such an obvious fact about Swinburne.

"Huuh? Turpitude? What's that mean?"

Sheldon glared at Max. "Well, for starters…shameful acts of vileness or depravity, criminal acts including murder…. Oh, I could go on and on!"

Max only smiled. "Point taken."

36

Proctor's office at Environ-Oil was right next door to Attorney and Chairman of the Board Harold R. Miller, not because he liked him; but because he couldn't think without him. Miller was his legal robot, validating every word, every sigh, and every half-formed sentence.

"We've got that little bastard W.D. on the run! Right, Harold?"

"Yes sir. Yes, we do, sir. Ah, as I was saying before you interrupted, the business of transporting crude petroleum, oil, their related products and derivatives including liquefied hydrocarbons, or natural gas by pipeline as a common carrier, is declared to be in the public interest and necessary to the public welfare," he stopped for a breath. "And the taking of private property therefore is declared to be for a public use and purpose."

"Oh my! Are you reading that from a script? Don't stop. Do I ever love to hear you say thooooose words."

"Ah, no. I have it memorized. Let me lay a little more on you, Proctor, to wit: Any corporation or association qualified to do business in the state of Minnesota engaged in or preparing to engage in the business of transporting crude petroleum, oil, their related products and derivatives including liquefied hydrocarbons, or natural gas by pipeline as a common carrier, is authorized to acquire, for the purpose of such business, easements or rights-of-way, over, through, under or across any lands, not owned by the state or devoted to public purpose for the construction, erection…laying, maintaining, operating, altering, repairing, renewing and removing in whole or in part, a pipeline for the transportation of crude petroleum, oil, their related products and derivatives including liquefied hydrocarbons, or natural gas."

"My God, Harold, did you say erection – in whole or in part? It's as if I wrote all this myself."

Harold was close to passing out from Proctors' frenzied vibes. He had to take a slight pause.

Proctor had never been this excited. None of his wives or girlfriends ever caused this kind of erection. OH! No. Not once.

Harold concluded his recitation:

"To such end it shall have and enjoy the right of eminent domain to be exercised in accordance with this chapter, and acts amendatory thereof, all of which provisions shall govern insofar as they may be applicable hereto. Nothing herein shall be construed as authorizing the taking of any property owned by the state, or any municipal subdivision thereof, or the acquisition of any rights in public waters except after permit, lease, license or authorization issued pursuant to law." He sneezed. It was all so goddamn boring.

"Proctor, where's that paperwork from the Two Crows on the appraised value of the land?"

"I don't know."

"No? Ahhhhh. Here it is."

"Go ahead, Harold, and file it as chairman of the board with Attorney General Lawrence Klinke."

Proctor stood up, grabbed his valise, making sure he had his ticket back to Las Vegas. He stared out the window at the traffic on Shepherd Road.

He had a vague feeling he'd forgotten something.

# # #

After spending a week in Las Vegas, Proctor was set to take a trip to Minnesota again. He arrived at the North Las Vegas Airport on Thursday morning; the sun was just coming up, and the chill of the desert air was subsiding. This was his favorite airport, the one he always looked forward to leaving from. After the maintenance check was completed on his Beechcraft Bonanza F33A and a flight plan filed, the adventure began: he would fly at an altitude of 11,500 feet to the Double Eagle II Airport, outside Albuquerque, for a fuel stop. This would get him all the way to the DuPage Airport near Chicago. He had two appointments there. He planned a stopover, a tie-down and refueling, before leaving the next day for the Grand Forks International Airport in North Dakota.

As he flew over the majestic Grand Canyon, he thought he saw a wolf pair running along the banks of the Colorado River. He squinted. No, it couldn't be. It must be a coyote pair. Oh God, he thought, why did I have to see them? They brought back a sharp uncomfortable pain in his chest, of that trophy hunt so many years ago, actually in the 50's, when, he, Sammy and Ully had a bet on who was the bravest, toughest, and most cunning; who was the real man amongst them?

It was Sammy's idea to go on a wolf kill. He'd heard about the Wolf Wars and told Proctor that it would get media attention. Now, after all that had happened, Proctor wondered if he would ever really forget that horrible hunting trip to Yellowstone National Park.

Ansel, their hunting guide, split them up – putting them each about a mile apart on separate deer stands.

After Proctor stopped playing around making deer and moose calls he settled down. He fiddled with his rifle for about an hour playing the big hunter peering through the branches and squinting up at the sun. Then he started to get bored.

A little later, he thought he heard a rustling sound. Was a creature moving around on the ground? He quietly loaded his rifle and readied himself. But he heard no more. After an hour, he was ready to call it quits; then he heard that noise again.

Something was walking and pushing, shoving, and scattering the bramble bushes. He decided to fire a couple of warning shots up into the trees.

He climbed down the deer stand ladder and ran straight into Sammy and Ansel.

"What the hell's going on here? Have you been firing up into the trees?" Ansel was staring at Proctor. "You nitwit."

"Ah, yes, I have – I thought I'd scare a wolf."

"You freaked out Ully, he's gone. He hiked back to the trail headquarters, I guess."

Ully later told Senior that Proctor tried to kill him and he pressed charges. No one saw any wolves at all.

# # #

Proctor, still lost in thought about that Yellowstone *dishabille*, flew into the DuPage Airport, near Chicago, by rote – almost in a dream state. He parked his plane and had it refueled and checked over. He took a car service into

Chicago to attend his meetings.

He stayed overnight in a nearby hotel arranged by the DuPage Flight Center. The next day he felt rested and soon regained his equilibrium and the day seemed calm weather-wise.

When he returned to the airport he was met by an elderly guard who quizzed him. "Mr. Swinburne, did you come out here last night to get something from your plane?"

"No, I did not. Did you see someone enter my plane or snoop around it?"

"Well, it was a shadowy presence; I really couldn't see anyone – but thought it might be you?"

This bothered Swinburne. "I want to see any surveillance photos you have. Right now!"

"Yes, sir." An hour later two security guards provided footage of the entire evening and nothing seemed out of place. Except, there was a shadow. After looking a second time, Swinburne decided to continue on his trip anyway.

After leaving Chicago, Swinburne headed north to Grand Forks International Airport. Although he'd noted that a light snowfall was forecast for the North Dakota/Minnesota border, he felt he could relax now. This was the last leg of his journey. He thought about his plane, so special to him, and all the high wire regional trips he'd made in it. He'd flown alone over the Grand Canyon, the Arizona Desert, the Salt Flats of Utah, and the Badlands of South Dakota.

An hour later, Swinburne flew over Polk County, Minnesota and made a descent into a lower airway to take a look at the property he planned to take by eminent domain. Oh, everything was coming together.

Suddenly the engine sputtered and lost power. Swinburne checked the engine instruments – nothing wrong. But he did notice a heavier than predicted tailwind. He decided to take the precaution of radioing the Air Route Traffic Control Center in Farmington that he might be in trouble. He might have to make an emergency landing and would need directions for a suitable clearing.

Soon, the plane started to shake and tremble and the engine stalled. He radioed the Air Traffic Control again.

"May Day, May Day, May Day. Pilot Swinburne N889RS about to force land near Trail, Minnesota. Need reply."

"Pilot Swinburne, we have you on the radar. Land at your discretion. Consult your sectional map for tree line in your area." He did and saw that he had more than a mile for landing. "Emergency equipment will be notified. How many passengers on board?"

"Just me – er – pilot R. Proctor Swinburne," he stammered as he successfully landed; but unexpectedly snapped a wing due to hitting a giant boulder encrusted with snow. The plane went into a slide with a lot of damage to the pilot's side of the plane. Swinburne was shook up, his hands cut from the glass and bleeding profusely. He climbed out the door opposite the pilot's side. Once on the ground, he fell to his knees, unable to stand. He did not hear the radio:

"May Day, May Day, May Day. Pilot Swinburne. Help is on the way. Reply."

#

Swinburne came around slowly, aware of a presence. He heard a wolf howl nearby. He opened his eyes and stared out into the black eyes of fifteen or more wolves that had ringed his body. He felt terror course throughout his body like no other time in his life. Why now? Oh, God. Why now when life was culminating into his greatest achievements?

The wolves came closer as a group and he could hear them growling. The large gray wolf stepped out and stood next to him. Swinburne was filled with remorse. He knew that once he'd tried to hunt wolves in Yellowstone National Forest. And for no good reason. He didn't hate them.

They all moved in closer as a group. He thought he saw pity in the big gray's eyes and then Swinburne screamed – "Heaven help me! Oh, God. Ohhhhhhh God." Were they going to eat him?

"No, noooooooo! Please, nooooooo."

Suddenly he experienced a violent shudder in his entire body and a deep pain in his chest as his heart stopped. It shook him beyond his fear. He seemed to float upward with the pain, like riding a wave. Was he leaving his body? Was he dying? Soon all went black and he slipped away to the netherworld that all dead occupy before their final release.

The wolves started howling. The alpha wolf looked at Swinburne's body and over at the fire flaring up all around the plane as fuel leaked from the busted wing. Then the wolves heard the sound of an engine in the sky. A medevac was about to land; its searchlights scanning the ground. The wolves knew it was time for them to leave. They all waited silently in single file for the alpha wolf to signal their departure. They circled the dead man's body, and one by one, leapt up and over him; secure in their survival and nature's redemption, heading for their home in the densely wooded area.

# # #

"I don't believe what I am looking at," said flight paramedic Justin Wilson. He was using his binoculars to stare out at the scene: Wolves' circling a body, then jumping over it. Then he saw them running single file into the woods receding into the moonlight, backlit by the flames consuming the plane. He looked over at pilot, Lars Overby who was also staring out at the jaw dropping scene: The body on the ground, close to flames rising from the plane – it looked dire.

" Ohhhhh! Are they leaving? Don't wolves eat people?"

"For God's sake, Lars! No, I've never heard of it. Well, let's say at least they're not eating this one."

"Well, just to be sure, let's pick up the pilot and get the hell out of here."

As Wilson departed the Bell 206 Long Ranger Helicopter, he ducked down to avoid being hit by the rotors, and it was then that he heard the far-off wolf howls. Soon there were many more wolves that joined in the howl, from all directions melding into a mighty wilderness chorus.

37

It was still snowing lightly as the medevac touched down on the Meritcare Hospital's rooftop heliport in Fargo, North Dakota. The copter landed smoothly on the helipad and three people standing by the doorway ran toward it in a crouching position to help unload the patient.

As the paramedic shifted the gurney for transport of the body of the unconscious man to the receiving trauma doctor, he felt a pang of sadness, who was this man? Why was he flying so low? Wilson couldn't get the image of the wolves out of his mind. He then looked over in surprise at two policemen standing sternly by the door to the elevator. Why were they here? He recognized the sheriff from Polk County, Roman Bahnrude, standing tight-lipped in the shadows. He knew this was no ordinary rescue.

The transfer was made quickly and the patient was on his way down one flight to the ER. The trauma doctor already had the patient fitted with an oxygen mask and two nurses had installed a port for an IV. There was a lot of commotion in ER as the staff hurriedly made plans for surgery and life giving protocol. Everyone worked quickly to save the life of this badly injured man.

"Do we have his ID?" Dr. Angus Shellum took charge.

"Yes, doctor, we do," Nurse Melissa Anderson read the report written by paramedic Wilson on the site. He had found a wallet with driver's license, medical emergency card and a passport at the scene of the crash. "It's R. Proctor Swinburne, age 57, of Oxnard, California," she hesitated, "blood type O Positive, diabetic, a personal doctor's address and telephone number, and, ah, a home address in Los Angeles."

"Start the blood transfusion immediately; he's lost a lot of blood – he's broken several ribs." Dr. Shellum was preparing for surgery. "Try to find his family – wife, relatives, and notify them of his critical condition." The nurses scattered quickly to do his bidding as a second trauma doctor, Dr. Michael Clark entered the room. "Here to aid and assist," he said and took his place beside Dr. Shellum.

Meanwhile Sheriff Bahnrude put in a radio call to W.D. Caldwell in Erskine. He knew the well-known realty agent had returned from California several days earlier. "Hey, W.D., get over here to Fargo, pronto," he said, "we've got a man here in critical condition by the name of R. Proctor Swinburne, someone you have met, I believe?"

"Uh, yes, that's correct. My God, what happened?"

"Airplane crash. Come quick. Meritcare ER. We might need your help with the press." He hung up.

In a matter of seconds, W.D. was out the door enroute to Fargo. He had just driven through Crookston and entered US Highway 10 when he was stopped by the highway patrol. He pulled over to the side of the road and rolled his window down.

"Good evening, Mr. Caldwell. Park your car in that driveway and come with me."

"Well, uh, I know I was speeding, but it's an emergency…I have to get to Fargo."

"Yes, I know. Sheriff Bahnrude has ordered me to bring you to Fargo. Please get in."

W.D. parked his car, got in the patrol car, and they took off, siren blaring, speeding up to 100 miles an hour. They slowed down as they entered metro Fargo and hit Broadway, delivering W.D. in record time to the Meritcare ER.

He joined Sheriff Bahnrude in one of the family rooms adjacent to the ER and received more detailed information about the crash. W.D. was horrified by what he heard: that Swinburne had crashed while flying low over the Olsen property near Trail. He wondered what he was doing there. He was reminded of his visit to Environ-Oil and the surprise at seeing a map of his property up on a wall along with a map of the nearby tank terminal in Clearbrook, Minnesota.

"What's the chance of his recovery?" W.D. was suddenly very upset.

"Pretty slim, I'd say." Sheriff Bahnrude's worried expression was reflected in the window facing downtown Fargo. It could be a long night.

#

It was early morning around 4:00 a.m. when Swinburne was wheeled back to a private room in the ER. He was swathed in bandages and hooked up to several monitors. A policeman stood outside the room as the medical team placed the patient in his bed.

"Keep a close watch on the patient, Sergeant," said Dr. Shellum who looked extremely concerned.

"Yes, doctor, I will." He watched as the doctor walked slowly down the hallway followed by nurses and technicians. He knew a new shift was now on board and he hoped the energy would ramp up, too.

"Hey, Arnold, has there been any change?" W.D. walked over to the door of the private room but did not enter.

"Well, frankly, I don't know anything, W.D. I'm just here to keep everyone out. But I guess there's a family member due any minute who has clearance to enter." W.D. took a chair behind the policeman and they chatted quietly for a few minutes.

W.D. then became aware of footsteps, someone walking quickly down the hallway headed their way. He stood up and looked, curious as to who was approaching. He was surprised to see a very small man, not just short, but diminutive – perhaps five feet tall – confidently striding toward him. He was wearing a black overcoat styled like a military greatcoat and high-heeled boots. He had on a black hat over his ginger-colored hair and was wearing tan gloves and carrying a small briefcase. He was accompanied by two stocky, dark complected men, who kept looking left and right.

The policeman stood up to greet the visitor. "Do you have an ID, sir?"

"Yes, here it is."

The small man tried to look past the policeman and into the room. W.D. thought this was the family member they'd been waiting for.

"Ahem, go in, sir." The policeman pushed the door open wider and reached in to turn on a light. The small man took off his coat and dropped it on the floor along with the briefcase. He ran over to the bed to Swinburne and cried out, "Proctor, Proctor, its Sammy – I'm here – and I'll stay with you until I can bring you home."

Suddenly Swinburne's eyes opened briefly and a smile played on his lips as if in recognition of the visitor. Then he lapsed back into unconsciousness. The small man continued to talk softly to him; he then put his arms around him and started to cry. He took off his suit jacket and then got into bed with the patient, still talking to him in a loving way.

#   #   #

All of the alarms were set off as the monitor stopped. Swinburne shuddered. He emitted a sigh as life eased away like a breeze into eternity.

The small man was aware of what had happened and he felt the change in the atmosphere. He knew Swinburne was dead. He became hysterical and uttered an unearthly wail.

W.D. was touched by this scene of devotion and deep caring between family members. He stood back as the ER team took over. The small man was helped up, but could not stand; staggering in his grief. Dr. Shellum stepped over to him and supported him on the left, while Nurse Anderson put her arms around his shoulders. They walked away, the small man keening in terrible paroxysms of grief.

Sheriff Bahnrude rounded the corner and was soon on the scene. He got a quick report from the policeman and then turned to W.D.

"I'm so sorry it had to end this way, but death was inevitable with such severe injuries."

"Yes, I am sorry, too. Was that Swinburne's brother?" W.D. was curious as he looked too old to be a son.

"Well, no. That's a boyhood friend. His name is Samuel C. Walberg, and he is the CEO of CBS Productions in Los Angeles."

W.D. was shocked; he'd heard that name many times in Los Angeles while working on the Tarintina case.

"What! Walberg?"

The sheriff continued, "Yeah, he arrived by private jet, had a BMW at the airport, and came straight over here."

W.D. was speechless as the sheriff continued: "Walberg is making all arrangements, accompanying the body to St. Paul for an autopsy, and then back to Oxnard for burial."

W.D. felt the irony of the Swinburne tragedy; all that ambition, yearning and striving, ending in death at an out of the way hospital amongst strangers. Was this an example of a man's reach exceeding his grasp?

38

It was past midnight and Chris Handler had the television on while working at his desk. Suddenly the program was interrupted by a news flash: *"This just in... millionaire executive R. Proctor Swinburne, dead from injuries suffered when his private plane crashed in the Minnesota wilderness. More details later."*

He was just finishing up a report for Walberg on the Tarintina assault in which R. Proctor Swinburne had played a part in the plot to kill the esteemed director.

Now he was shocked and conflicted. Handler put the papers back in the file, cleaned off the top of his desk, and stood up wondering what to do. He couldn't write that report now that clearly indicated that everything pointed to Swinburne as the suspect in an attempted murder case

The dead were never prosecuted.

Just then the telephone rang. He reached over to pick up the extension. "Handler here. Huh? No? Are you sure? What time will that be? Yeah. That's all verrrry interesting. Thanks for calling."

The call was from one of the tipsters, calling in to report that Samuel E. Walberg, their client, who'd paid so much money to the firm to investigate the attempted murder of Tarintina, had just been on television talking about the loss of Swinburne, a boyhood friend. He'd been with him at his death and would escort the body back to Oxnard, California for funeral services. The tipster also reported that through his sources he'd found out that Walberg was the executor of Swinburne's will and the chief beneficiary of his estate.

Handler had a lot to think about. Swinburne dead? The shock was too much. He stepped over to his bar stocked with the most exquisite liquors. But he chose a whiskey, poured a small glass, drinking it down in a few gulps. Then he poured another and walked down the stairs to his patio sipping as he went. He had to take a break. There was nothing more calming than his view of the ocean; watching the waves roll in and out could wash away a lot of stress and confusion.

# # #

An hour later, Handler was back at his desk. The respite had put the report in perspective and now his mind was clear as to how it should be written. He shut the television off and rearranged his files. The first one contained the testimony of seven witnesses who said they'd heard Aldean Matheson say "I'm going to kill Tarintina."

He felt it was best to charge Matheson with the assault. Another file was opened that indicated why he'd made that threat. A key executive at CBS, who did not want his name used, reported that Tarintina had made a low ball offer on the rights to Matheson's book on the illegal growing of marijuana in Shasta-Trinity National Forest. He heard Matheson demand a higher fee and Tarintina agreed to the sum and went to Walberg, CEO, to sign off on the new offer. Walberg refused and Tarintina's original offer stood.

Matheson declined the offer, pulled the book, and filed a law suit against CBS Productions. Tarintina turned around and bought the rights to an Indian Gaming book by Matheson without Walberg and CBS. About two months later, Tarintina also bought the rights to a bestseller by Matheson on the oil fields of Los Angeles without Walberg or CBS involvement.

"What the hell?" Handler was confused by these facts. Was Tarintina going into production on his own?

There must be another reason Matheson had it in for Tarintina. He looked back into the Handler Posse file and saw that at one time Tarintina had an affair with Joyce Santa Anna. But that was quite awhile ago. Why put a message on his phone now that he was going to kill him?

He reviewed the phone messages retrieved by the LAPD from that Friday evening of the assault. Yes, there it was. 5:15 p.m. As he continued to read the file he saw that Matheson was already on his way to LAX arriving at 5:00 p.m. with a female companion. They'd checked in immediately for a flight to LaGuardia International Airport and a connecting limo ride to Montauk, Long Island. Had someone else made that call?

He continued to review the files. Briefly he looked over the info on the gray Saab driven by the attackers. LAPD found that it was stolen Thursday evening from the parking lot of the Burbank Community Theatre. Its owner was Jason Sanborn, director of the theatre, who'd reported it missing at 9:00 p.m. They found the gray Saab early Saturday morning burned to a crisp in an empty lot near South Central.

A tipster had called in information about an older relative – an uncle – who'd spent time in prison who was employed by Swinburne, along with a prison sidekick, to do his dirty work. They'd been seen assisting Swinburne on a number of occasions. They were mentioned by name in a report by a Minnesota sheriff as wanted for questioning in the kidnapping of a young boy in Erskine, Minnesota. Handler felt the description of the two men who'd arrived at Tarintina's residence, as seen on the courtyard camera, fit the henchmen described by the tipster.

He finalized his report for Walberg by making up a case against Aldean Matheson: He'd set up the attack on Tarintina to teach him a lesson. He'd hired thugs to scare him. Handler included the death certificate for Aldean Matheson and advised no further effort be made to pursue the findings of his report or to make it public as per an agreement with the Matheson Estate.

Handler went back down to the courtyard. He'd written the report just like his Uncle Herschel taught him – basically always protect your client's interest. It was time for a glass of prosecco. In his heart of hearts, he knew the assault on Tarintina had been planned by R. Proctor Swinburne. He'd heard firsthand about Swinburne's efforts to finagle W.D. out of his property in a land grab for a proposed pipeline. He knew that by getting rid of Tarintina there would be no documentary revealing the secrets of his company. He would be secure in his dream of becoming a billionaire oil tycoon.

# # #

Handler felt he'd done the right thing by changing the report. He'd earned his fee in more ways than one. He sat back and stared down at the breaking waves along Malibu Beach. He was deeply puzzled by Walberg and why he'd hired him to investigate who'd attacked Wade Tarintina. He must have known it was planned by R. Proctor Swinburne. Handler didn't know they were boyhood friends – closer than brothers?

He watched the tide come in – it was so much like life – roiling emotions such as love, hate, greed, and revenge, washed over by the ocean waters; unseen, until the tide went out revealing the detritus of those thoughts and feelings.

Sometimes there was a heavy price to pay.

39

"Good mornin' ma'am. May I help you?" I smiled at the well-groomed tall man wearing a starched white jacket who'd answered the door chimes at the mansion in Benedict Canyon. Obviously he was Wade Tarintina's butler.

"Why yes, I'm an employee of Mr. Tarintina's. I was just driving by and thought he might like a hello in person."

"Well, he hasn't had much company as of late." He opened the door wider and dipped down in a bow to welcome me into the parlor.

I was just amazed by the beauty of the room; the crystal chandelier appeared to be antique and set everything off to best advantage. Wade really had a gorgeous environment.

"May I have your name, ma'am? I will check with Wade to see if he's accepting visitors."

"Oh, of course – my name is Dyanna Dahlberg and I work at CBS Productions."

He stepped away disappearing behind a door. Soon he returned. "Yes, he would like to see you. Just go through that door he's out there in the garden."

"Thank you," I said. I walked over to the door, opened it, and took a step. I was so shocked by what I saw I could not proceed.

There in that beautiful garden with lovely peonies and pansies, a shimmering pool in the background, sat a skeletal human form, arms wasted, and fingers boney. It was a man, but just barely. His hair was missing in patches and his skin was red and scaly. He was seated in a wheelchair with a soft blanket over his knees and a white towel around his shoulders. It was Wade Tarintina or what was left of him.

He smiled at me, a semblance of his charm and personality flashing for a moment. Then it disappeared.

"Dyanna, it is so lovely of you to visit me. I suppose you've heard what's happened to me?" He weakly made an effort to push a chair my way.

"Ah, no, Wade, I haven't heard anything at all. I was just driving by and thought of you, as I often do, and decided you might like a drop-in visitor." I found it hard to look at him. I sat down in the chair across from him, somewhat caught off guard.

Wade realized my predicament and with his gracious manner started to give me some background. "Well, I'm dying of lung cancer. I don't have long left."

He stopped to see how I reacted to this.

"Wade, I am so shocked. No one at CBS has the slightest inkling that you're ill, let alone, have cancer."

I stood up and stepped over to him; I knelt down and put my arms around him. "Wade, so many people, including me, care about you, and love you…is there anything I can do? Call medical specialists – anything to help you?"

I started crying as I continued to hold him. I just couldn't imagine the loneliness of facing something like this.

"Oh! Dyanna, you have a good heart – I know that. But I've been everywhere, including the Mayo Clinic." Wade wiped a tear from his eye. "I have been helped by my cousin

Ivor, he's moved in here to wait on me hand and foot. Ah, he's taking a break from his musical career and…."

Just then the door opened and Ivor pushed a trolley in with a pot of tea, cups, and a variety of small cookies. I was taken aback by the comparison with my first visit to Wade's office at CBS and the coffee offered to me on a cart from his assistant.

"I am kept quite busy – my energy is limited to just an hour or two a day in writing a script based on Aldean's book of the Los Angeles oil fields."

Wade then began to tell me the inner workings of the documentary and how close he was to finishing it. I was impressed by his quick, perceptive mind and how much he had accomplished.

Then he told me something I'd never forget: "Dyanna, I have lung cancer. I have it because I grew up in the projects of Baldwin Hills. I lived many years next to a pump jack owned by Environ-Oil," he seemed very tired, "they began fracking or acidization when the oil became hard to access. All this occurred just a few feet from my front door…and the fumes have shortened my life."

"Wade, let me help you. Do you need research? Interviews? Anything at all? Please call on me."

"Thank you, Dyanna…I'll do that. I need to tell my story before it's too late." Suddenly his head fell back, his eyes closed; the lights in his great mental stage were dimming.

Ivor quickly stepped in to wrap him in another blanket, administer medication, and take him inside and down a hallway.

I decided to leave quietly. My car was outside in the courtyard. I asked the driver to take me to my home instead of back to CBS productions. I knew I could not face my co-workers. Suddenly I realized that I recognized Ivor. He was a great blues singer, one I'd seen in concert about a year ago. Now I admired him even more.

    The main reason I'd stopped in to see Wade was because I was leaving CBS and Los Angeles. I'd wanted to thank him for all he'd done for me. Now my heart was heavy and I had so much to think about. I could show my love for him by working on his documentary. Would that help sustain him in the days ahead?

40

"I still believe it was murder," said Max. It was now two months after the death of R. Proctor Swinburne and the duo was returning from Oxnard where Max had met with Swinburne's attorney.

"Yeah, I agree, it just couldn't have been an accident," said Sheldon shaking his head vehemently. "But, I just don't know who – or what – did it?"

There was genuine grief in their voices as they talked about the Boss: "It sure was strange not to have a funeral."

Max recalled the memorial service at Environ-Oil: just a few friends and family members present.

"It seemed so disrespectful," Sheldon said. "Also the reading of the will was so casual."

"Yeah, we all knew his wife Meghan Masters would get just about everything and his son would get all the rest." Max frowned, "I was surprised to learn Sammy was the executor, though, and beneficiary of Environ-Oil, weren't you?"

"No, not really. What did you think of his reading that poem, 'So We'll Go No More A Roving,' as a tribute to the Boss? Kinda cool, huh?" Sheldon was impressed.

"Ah, it seemed awfully sad. Like a goodbye from the grave."

"Maybe it was a poem from their college days? Sammy said it was written by Lord Byron."

"Yeah, could be. Well, I really liked it, too. You know Sammy and Proctor were tight. Sammy was Proctor's wingman. They used to go roving around, chasing women, and just having loads of fun."

"Huh? I think it was Sammy that could've used a wingman. He doesn't have anything much to attract the ladies."

"Yeah, I agree. But he was a good friend and the only person to drop everything and come to Proctor's bedside when he was dying."

"Yeah, I heard that."

They drove along in silence reflecting on how their life would change now that the Boss was gone.

After a while, Sheldon looked over at Max with serious concern. "When do you sign the deed on that La Brea oil field that Proctor left you?"

Max slowed the Town Car down. "I guess next week. Sammy set up a meeting with the lawyer. You know you're getting fifty percent of it?"

"Jeez. I am so damned grateful, Max. You know I'll keep up my end of the bargain. Uh, filing taxes, overseeing the accounting service and all legal ramifications as per our agreement. Uh, don't you?"

Max nodded as he took a left turn off the freeway to Calabasas. "Yeah, you are *mishpacha* now." They drove into the setting sun; the warm orange rays warming their faces.

Sheldon sighed and gently closed his eyes. Max cleared his throat and smiled. Oh, life was good.

41

It was Saturday morning and the snow lay in heavy drifts around Gunhilde's mobile home in McIntosh, Minnesota. Her deck was unrecognizable and the skeletal trees in back of the trailer seemed lonely. Maxwell, her Manx cat, refused to step out into the white desolation. While holding the door for him to make up his mind, she saw her sister Anita drive up.

"Oh, Anita, I am so glad to see you. I think I'm going back to California as soon as I can," she was close to tears. "This weather!"

"Oh, yes, let's go back." Anita stepped gingerly through a drift, her boots covered in snow. She'd left the car along the road.

"I've got the coffee on and I've made some *lefse* and *krumkaka* cookies."

"Well, my goodness, you sure made it worth my while to stop in," Anita giggled as she entered the cozy kitchen with its warm, delicious scent of baking.

Gunhilde poured two cups of coffee and plated up the Norwegian delicacies.

"You know, I will just never forget our lovely trip to Los Angeles," said Anita. She picked up a framed photo of Dyanna and gave it a kiss. They both lifted their coffee cups in toast to her.

"I guess I'm still in shock that Dyanna quit her job at CBS productions, aren't you?"

"Yes and no. Frankly, I think she needs a man in her life. I have to admit, I thought she'd be engaged by now to Raymond Siqueiros. You know he lives in California…well, northern California. But that's not very far when you're in love."

"Ah, no it's not. But then I never thought he had a chance with her after the way he up and left. She claimed she had no idea why he abruptly fled after only a few days here. My, he sure was good-looking," Gunhilde smiled as she thought of his courtly ways.

"Yeah, true, but I think Chris Handler is more handsome… and way richer."

"Hmmmm, guess I have to agree. Wonder how that romance will go now that she's quit her job?"

"Say, maybe it's going so well that it's the reason she quit her job?"

Gunhilde had to laugh. "Oh, Anita, you never cease to amaze me…and you may be right."

They were silent for awhile, both deep in thought.

"I must say, I've changed my opinion of W.D. Caldwell. Pretty smart old guy – maybe his real talent is wasted here in the sticks?"

"Yes, I'd agree, Anita. But I think he chooses to live here in Minnesota. It's a family thing."

"Yes, I believe he comes from a long line of Norwegian ancestors. I wonder if any of them were detectives."

"Oh, speaking of detectives, did you see the latest TV coverage about the murder of that famous writer?"

"No, I didn't. What was it?"

"Well, I guess his girl friend, mother of his baby boy, almost died, too. Shock or something. Oh, it was so tragic…because they'd made plans to get married in a few weeks."

"Life is so cruel," Anita was puzzled. "I wonder how all that could have happened like that?"

"It seemed like I remember that another woman was involved – maybe a former girlfriend or wife?"

Anita looked at Gunhilde. "Well, look no further. She did it. Is she in custody?"

"I don't know. But she should be."

Then Gunhilde changed the subject. "I can't wait for the hollyhocks to bloom in the spring."

Just then there was scratching on the door. Maxwell wanted out. He'd finished his *lefse* and could use some exercise. Maybe there was rabbit or two he could chase.

#   #   #

A few miles away, in Erskine, Lance was shuffling along over the snow drifts on his new snowshoes. They were his Christmas present from the W.D.'s and he'd quickly learned how to use them. He was on his way to the realty office by the back way and the scenery was exciting – hills looked like mountains and the lake was covered in white flakes.

He was ten now and W.D. said he could drink coffee; but it had to be decaffeinated. He wondered what it would be like when he was grown up. Would he still be here in this small town?

He looked up at the sun and saw how it caused the snow to sparkle and the ground looked so white and pure. He remembered what W.D. told him about his trip to Los Angeles and how he investigated a case that involved the bad side of the oil business. He looked down at his snowshoes wondering if a pipeline flowed under him. Was it a dark shadowy river of black, smelly gunk? The kind that threatened the water they drank and the rich soil for the crops and their gardens?

He'd asked W.D. about oil. He knew that Uncle Max and Uncle Sheldon had grabbed him because they wanted W.D. to sign his land away for a pipeline. He also knew that his papa had died in a pipeline ditch. He hated that word: oil. He'd asked W.D. how it came about…where did it come from? W.D. told him it lay deep in the ground and was formed maybe 65 million or more years ago from the bodies of dead animals and plants. Did dinosaur bones get mixed up in the oil? Yes, W.D. said it was possible. He said mankind had used oil for thousands of years. But a man in Pennsylvania figured out how to dig an oil well in 1859. It was a commodity that owners of pipelines and oil fields now made a lot of money from.

What would happen when the oil fields ran dry? What then?

Little did he know that his question bothered experts and scientists, too.

42

The busy day was coming to an end. W.D. had been researching information on how to set up a nature conservancy on the Steve Olsen estate. He wanted to make sure there would never be a pipeline running across the acreage and the land trust seemed the best bet. He'd had a close call when Swinburne set his sights on his property. Now he was gone, but no doubt, there'd be another pipeline company that would attempt to buy or take the land by *eminent domain*.

He planned to build a park called *Swinburne's Nature Retreat and RV Campground* in honor of the first bid on the land. He was going to open a three- month seasonal camp site for boating, hiking, and fishing without an entry fee. Just one request: No smoking. Maybe special tours for wolf sightings? And bears, too?

"Hon, why name the retreat after Swinburne?"

"Oh, I think it's *homage* to defeating the pipeline grab. Returing the land to its original purpose."

He stood up. He was getting ready to leave his office when Lance called out, "Mr. W.D, there's an urgent telephone call from the United Kingdom from a Ms. Dahlberg."

W.D. returned to his desk and picked up the telephone, not sure what to expect. "My gosh, Dyanna, so good to hear from you. Are you okay? What are you doing in the UK?"

"Well, W.D. It's a long story, but a friend of mine needs your help."

"Uh, tell me about it."

"Professor Raymond Siqueiros from UC Berkeley is here teaching at Cambridge University and has gotten himself involved in the murder of one of his students."

"Why? How?"

"Well, he was dating her. Ah, it seems she was found dead – a homicide – in the early morning hours, on the bank of the River Cam. He swears he walked her back to the dorm after their date. In fact, she'd signed in around midnight and there was no record of her leaving again."

"Sounds strange. Dyanna, you know I am not a licensed investigator. It would be best if you contacted Chris Handler in Malibu to take this on."

"Oh, yes, I know. Actually I'm travelling with Chris Handler now. We stopped here for a couple of days on our way to Milan." There was a pause on the line and then he heard the voice of Chris Handler.

"Greetings, W.D. I'd like you to work for me again. I've been hired by Cambridge University to look into the murder of a young female student. How do you feel about doing some recon at the university as a retired don – ah, that's a retired tutor or lecturer?"

"Oh," W.D. smiled. "Hmm, that's quite a stretch…a retired don. Sounds like fun, Chris."

He quickly realized his gaffe and said, "Oh my, what a tragedy." Then he quickly followed up. "Yes, I'm available. I know the drill. When I receive the deputization, check, and kit, I'll be ready to travel. Just name the date."

"Oh, W.D. so glad you can do this. Thank you. Dyanna's

professor friend is just beside himself with grief and shock. I will take care of all the details. Ah, bring your wife. We both send you our love and best wishes." He hung up.

W.D. sat back in his chair and took out one of his cigars. He was thinking of his last investigation in Los Angeles after Dyanna had joined CBS Productions. Now here she was in London. Something told him she was the harbinger of another adventure.

"Oh, Renee," he called out, "I say, my lady, we're going to London for a few days."

Just then, Lance looked up from polishing the door knob, "I think I might be bloody well ready to help out on this investigation, too, Mr. W.D."

Renee, looked up from the typewriter, rolled her eyes, and kept on typing.

-End-

SPECIAL THANK YOU TO:

Connie Knutson
Gerald Wade Varney
Dr. Martha Grandits
Vicky Trepanier
Anthony Swann
Janet Holley
Phil Hodapp
Paul Stolen

*A special fond remembrance of Milton Glaser,
a wonderful friend, a superb human and a creative wonder.*